skeins

stories by women

Published by Linen Press, London 2024
8 Maltings Lodge
Corney Reach Way
London W4 2TT
www.linen-press.com
© Linen Press 2024

Editors: Avril Joy, Aurelia Knight, Lynn Michell, Jess Richards, Sally J Morgan, Rebeccca Pitt.

Cover design: Lynn Michell
Cover image: Unsplash, Eugenia Maximova
Typeset by Zebedee
Printed by Lightning Source
ISBN: 978-1-7394431-0-8

Contents

Away with the Fairies

Anna Sansom

Granny was eighty-six when she trapped her first fairy. She held the sealed jar aloft, her pale eyes sparkling, thin lips split into a wide grin. Her tongue prodded her dentures into position before she spoke. 'Lookie!' she called out to us, her voice sounding like a toddler with a forty-a-day habit. 'Lookie here. Isn't she pretty?' Mum and I glanced at each other as she triumphantly replaced her prize on the windowsill. 'Wow, Granny,' I said. 'You'll be needing a cuppa now, I reckon.'

We formed a slow, shuffling procession to the common room where the nursing home staff had laid out ready-poured cups of tea and plates of mixed biscuits. We sat in a line on the high-backed, vinyl-clad chairs as we dunked and slurped. Granny didn't mention the fairy again that visit, preferring instead to reminisce about the summer holiday when Grandad got stuck in the sinking mud of an empty reservoir and she almost left him to perish.

I went back to visit the following week and found Granny asleep on her bed. Her windowsill was now filled with glass jars, stacked two storeys high. Each had a label stuck on with a name written in her spidery hand. She stirred and her watery eyes took a moment to register me. 'Sally?'

'Hi, Granny. What's all this then?' I pointed to the windowsill.

She gave a small cackle that turned into a cough, and I went over to help her sit upright. 'My fairies,' she said once she had caught her breath. 'I'm collecting them.'

'What are you collecting them for?'

Granny looked over to the door of her room. 'Close that will you, love?' Then, 'Don't tell your mother.' I nodded. 'I'm going to sell them. On eBay. You'll help me, won't you, love?'

'I'm not sure you can sell fairies on the internet, Granny.'

'Of course you can! If young women can sell their virginity, I'm sure you can sell my fairies.'

'Where did you hear about women selling their virginity?'

'William read it in the paper.'

'William? Which one is he?'

'Fat man. Big sausage fingers. He reads the paper every day and we help him with the crossword. I got a good one yesterday: *buccaneer*. Phyllis and I tell him all the answers. I think he likes the attention.'

'And he told you about eBay?'

Granny eased her legs over the side of the bed and worked her feet into her slippers. 'Yes, and whatshisname, the male nurse. He said his wife is an expert at it. She sells their kiddies' toys and clothes when they grow out of them. She made thirty pounds last month.' She paused while she concentrated on standing up. 'They sold a paddling pool.'

'Right, I see. And what are you thinking of charging for your fairies?'

'I don't really know. If we called them rare and unusual, limited edition... What do you reckon? A tenner each?'

I glanced over at the window and did a quick count. 'So, you'd be looking at about a hundred and forty quid. That's not bad.'

Granny took a wobbly step forward and grasped my hand. I felt her cool, papery skin press against my warm, resilient flesh. 'I'll give you a cut.' She tried to wink but it came out as a slow blink, giving the impression she was communicating with a secret code.

'I'll have to look into it. Check out eBay's terms and conditions. I don't think they sell virgins anymore. In the meantime, maybe you've got enough fairies for now? You've run out of space to keep them.' We stood hand-in-hand, surveying her spoils.

She shrugged. 'Perhaps. Still plenty of them out there, though,' she gestured towards her window and the jar-obscured view of the communal garden. 'Is it teatime?'

We had our tea on the patio, facing the big weeping willow that trailed its leafy fingertips across the neatly mown lawn. We'd had a tree like that at our old family home. My sisters and I used to make a camp under the dense, cascading foliage. The ground was always dry underneath, and we would place little offerings at the base of the trunk for the sprites and fairies we were sure lived there. My oldest sister, Debbie, would take the table and chairs from the doll's house and set them up like a miniature parlour. Leanne, the middle one, decorated it with flowers she collected from the garden. As the youngest, my role was to sing the magic song that would summon the otherworldly beings. It was a song that Granny had taught us from when we were in the crib. She said that her grandmother had sung it to her – and she was part fae.

We knew we always had to offer some food to the fairies and so each of us would save a little bit of our pudding for them. After dinner, we rushed out to fill the aged acorn cups we'd found in the woods with chocolate mousse or strawberry yoghurt or a bit of the inside of a custard cream. Fairies prefer sweet soft stuff, Granny said. Then we had to leave them to it, closing the willow curtain behind us and resisting the urge to peer through the gaps for a glimpse of their tell-tale sparkles and glitter.

When we went back the next morning, the chairs were often overturned and the acorn cups licked clean, proving that the fairies had partied in our makeshift lounge. As thanks for our gifts, Granny told us, they would grant us each a wish. We screwed our faces tight and clasped our hands as though in prayer as we whispered our secret yearnings under the cover of the big tree.

It wasn't a surprise that it had taken Granny eighty-six years to catch one. The fairies were usually shy and wily. 'How did you do it, Granny,' I asked as we drank our tea.

'I got old,' she replied. 'And they got lazy. They stopped trying to hide from me. They decided I was no longer a threat.' She chuckled and then reached into her mouth with her free hand to finger her false teeth.

'Do you need those fixed?'

'There's no point now,' she said.

I took a slow sip, choosing my words. 'Granny, I'm not sure it's a good idea to catch the fairies.'

'Of course, it's not. They're mad at me now,' she gave a little giggle. 'But they'll be gone soon anyway. Make us a bit of spare cash so we can go out for fish and chips. You, me, and Phyllis. Maybe William too if we get enough money. We'll make a day of it. Go to the seaside and paddle.'

'Is that what you want, Granny? To go to the sea? I could take you anyway, you know? And I can pay for it.'

'Find out about eBay.' Granny did another of her eight things. 'If you sell them all, we can have ice cream too.'

I phoned Debbie when I got home. Granny had said not to tell Mum, but she hadn't said anything about involving my sister. Debbie listened without interruption as I described the rows of assorted jars, their name tags, and Granny's insistence that we try to get some money for them. 'People sell farts in jars,' she concluded, 'so why not make-believe fairies?'

'Because I'm not one hundred percent sure that Granny *is* playing make-believe. What if she really thinks she's catching fairies?' I paused for Debbie to interject but she stayed quiet. 'What if she *can* actually see them?'

Debbie snorted. 'Don't be silly. I think it's way more likely she's losing her marbles than suddenly seeing fairies, don't you?' This time I was the one who stayed quiet. 'Oh, come on, Sally. She's winding you up.'

'She wants me to take her for fish and chips at the sea.' I was surprised to feel my throat tighten and my eyes smart as I spoke. 'I think it's, like, her last wish or something.' I couldn't hide the emotion in my voice.

Granny had never asked to go to the seaside before. I didn't think she even liked the sea. Ever since Grandad's near miss at the reservoir, she'd avoided anywhere with sinking sand and variable water levels. She used to tell us tales of giant octopuses that would grip our ankles and pull us into the deep if we stepped into the water. She said their suckers were so strong they could drag a whole boat down. So, to say she wanted to go for a paddle was a bit of a surprise. The fish and chips bit I could understand: the nursing home never gave them chips.

'You could just take her.' I could tell Debbie didn't want to dwell on the implications of my 'last wish' statement. Granny had always been such a big part of our lives, and still was, even though we could only see her during the designated visiting hours now.

'But what about all the jars?'

'I don't know. Take them away. Tell her you've eBayed them. Whatever. *Don't* try and sell them, though. You'll get done for trade description.'

9

The following week, I lifted a box full of Granny's jars out of the boot of my car and left them in the narrow hallway of my flat. I'd assured her that I'd list them that weekend. We'd agreed that they'd likely sell like hotcakes, and I could put a minimum bid of seven pounds plus postage. I didn't like lying to her, but Debbie said she'd read something about it being better to collude with someone with dementia than to insist on making them accept reality. I'd pointed out that we had no evidence that Granny had dementia. Her body may be frail, but her mind was sharp. She was still a whiz at crosswords. She'd come up with the eBay plan all on her own. 'But she is eighty-six,' Debbie replied, as though that alone explained it all.

I stubbed my toe on the box three times in one day, cursing and hopping each time. The third time, I sat on the floor beside the box to rub my bruised foot. *Maybe I should check on the fairies?* It was a ridiculous thought. I pulled a jar from the box and held it up to catch the light. I could just put the whole lot into the recycling, take Granny to the sea, and that would be the end of it. I brought the jar close to my mouth, 'What do you think I should do?' I whispered. Then I pressed the cool glass to my ear as if it was a conch shell and I was listening for the ocean.

Granny had always taught us to be respectful of the fairies. Our willow fairy parlour had only lasted one summer but I could still remember how it felt to look for magic and to believe it was there, whether I saw it or not. If Granny had trapped fairies in these jars, wouldn't they be hungry? And she'd said they were angry with her, too. The thought of a box of irate and starving fairies in my flat was unnerving. I replaced the jar and folded the cardboard flaps over the top. Maybe it wasn't just Granny who was losing it?

I had a packet of unopened Bourbon biscuits in the

10

kitchen. I turned the pack over in my hands for a few moments, feeling the ridges of the rounded corners pressing against the smooth cellophane wrapper. 'This is stupid,' I muttered as I took a knife to the top of the pack and slit it open. I carefully prised apart four biscuits, exposing their soft, chocolatey centres, and lay them on the countertop. Then I went back to the hall to retrieve the box. 'Right, you lot. This is my just-in-case insurance. If you're in there, don't be mad at me.' I selected the first jar from the box. 'And don't try to escape. Please.' I got a bit of the chocolate filling on the end of my knife, unscrewed the lid and lifted it a tiny bit, then quickly scraped the knife into the small space I'd made. The buttercream stuck to the inside of the rim, and I screwed the lid back on tight. Having done it for one, now I had to do it for all the others. 'Look what you've done to me, Granny. Debbie would be in stitches if she could see me now.' All done, I repacked the box and returned it to the hall.

I was about to head out when my phone rang. 'Granny's had a turn,' Debbie said as soon as I picked up. 'Mum says we have to go to the home. We need to get there ASAP, Sally,' she added, her voice sharp with worry.

'I'm on my way,' I said, grabbing my car keys and scooping up the box as I went. I plonked it on the passenger seat beside me. 'Please, please, please,' I repeated as I drove. 'Please let Granny be okay.'

Debbie was already waiting for me by the time I got to the home. She flagged me down in the car park and I stuck my head out of my open window. 'The ambulance has been and gone,' she said. 'They've taken Granny to the hospital. Mum went with her. I said I'd wait for you.'

'Should we go too?' My engine was still running.

'Mum said she'd call me. Poor Granny.' Debbie glanced at the box beside me. 'What's that?'

'Granny's fairies.'

'Oh, Sally. Really? I thought you were going to chuck them.'

'No, I fed them.'

Debbie looked at me incredulously. 'You didn't?'

'I think we should put them back. Back in the garden where Granny found them. Will you help me?'

Debbie glanced at her silent phone. 'Mum's going to call any moment.'

'I'll be quick.' I pulled the key from the ignition. 'I promise I'll be quick,' I repeated as I stepped out of the car and opened the passenger side.

We took the path that led around the building and into the garden. The willow's branches had been trimmed into a skirt that stopped about a metre from the ground and we ducked underneath. I put the box on the dusty soil and reached for a jar, glancing at the name Granny had written as I took off the lid. I gently placed the open jars at my feet and tossed the lids back into the box. Once I'd completed the task, I paused for a moment, listening to the willow sighing in the slight breeze.

'Okay now?' Debbie interrupted.

'Just a moment longer.' I clasped my hands and closed my eyes, making one more wish.

The ringing phone startled us both.

Deer Sightings

Susan Clegg

I was pregnant for the first time and on the way to Rome when I saw the deer. It was our last trip before we had to grow up and be parents and we'd planned as much high-living as I could manage at 30 weeks. But it started badly and got worse, much like the marriage itself. At the end of both, I wondered why we'd done it in the first place; none of it seemed real. But the baby inside me was real and so were the deer.

A crash up ahead on the motorway put us in a miles long tailback, and the flight had already boarded by the time we reached the airport. We pleaded with the check-in staff and made much of my gravid state, but they wouldn't let us on. 'If she miscarries because of stress,' Alex hissed as we gathered up our luggage, 'I'm suing each and every one of you.'

The next flight was early in the morning and it was too late to go home. We left the car where it was, in a far-flung car park, and set off for the nearest hotel on foot. Alex had most of the bags and he cursed airlines, motorways and travelling in general for the entire length of a road that had no other pedestrians on it and ended in a bleak concrete box of a hotel.

We had a clean room with a soft bed though, and I slept almost immediately, drifting down through the flickering TV light as Alex channel hopped.

I woke up earlier than I needed to, bright June sunlight sifting through the curtains. Alex was still sleeping, one fist clenched around the pillow as if he was angry even when unconscious. The room was already hot and I got up to open the window. But the catch had some kind of security device to stop it opening more than an inch or two, so I leaned into the narrow gap to get some cool air on my face.

There was a building site on this side of the hotel. I'd noticed the sign as we walked up the road the night before – *Terminal House – contemporary office space coming soon* – and it made me smile. 'Sounds more like a care home,' I'd said to Alex and he nodded and smiled back for a moment. From the window, I could see the flattened square of earth that would be the building's footprint and the start of the lift shaft in its centre. There was a weathered-looking Portakabin at the far side with an assortment of diggers behind it. As I stood there, something moved behind the Portakabin. I waited. Another shadow crossed a big yellow digger and then two deer emerged, fragile as twigs against the hulking machinery. They stepped delicately into the cleared space, paused for a moment to look around, then picked their way in my direction.

The site looked completely bare to me, but something must have been growing. They nosed the ground and tugged daintily from time to time at whatever it was they found. In the quiet of the early morning, I could hear tiny ripping sounds as they pulled the plants from the earth.

I turned to shake Alex awake. 'Look at this,' I whispered. 'There are deer outside.'

He hauled himself across the bed and swept back the curtain before I could stop him. The deer jerked up their heads, stared at us for a second, then bolted back towards the Portakabin, white rumps bobbing urgently.

'That's a design flaw,' Alex said and mimed pulling back a bow and arrow. 'Running target, that white arse.' His fingers flared to let the arrow fly.

There was a puff of dust and the deer disappeared.

Alex yawned. 'Come on then,' he said. 'Let's catch this fucking plane.'

Over the next few years Alex and I fought and separated and came back together and fought again. I thought about the deer sometimes and how they foraged so gracefully amongst the brutal machinery and razed earth. That moment of tranquility was something I held on to when things were bad.

Martha was six when the deer appeared at school. I was pregnant again, by a man who wasn't Alex. I had practically nothing left you could call a marriage. The daily routine of taking Martha to school and picking her up again was the only dependable thing there was.

She came home one day with a letter headed: WARNING. It went on to say that a deer had been seen in the woods behind the school; that this was a wild animal with unpredictable behaviour and possibly unknown diseases; and not to approach it under any circumstances.

I felt a stab of happiness. 'Have you seen it?' I asked Martha.

She shook her head. 'Miss Greaves says it might be dangerous.'

I laughed. 'Well, Miss Greaves is a stupid old fool. It'll be more scared of us than we are of it. Shall we see if we can find it? This Saturday morning when there's nobody at school?'

She looked anxious; she's an anxious child. 'But we aren't allowed to.'

'Yes, we are,' I said. 'No one can stop us.'

It was only just light when we left the house. Alex was asleep in the living room and I watched him while Martha put on her shoes. He lay across the sofa like a saggy mattress, one pale bare foot propped on the coffee table. I hadn't seen him for two days and I had no idea where he'd been, but that's how things were with us then.

The click of the front door was too loud and I thought I heard him call out. But we were off already, hurrying round the corner towards the school.

Martha held my hand and skipped along as she always did, but there was a worried look about her. As the school gates came in sight she skipped more and more slowly until she came to a complete stop.

'OK, Martha?'

She stared at the ground and shook her head.

'Shall we see if we can find the pretty deer?'

Another shake of the head.

'Well, that's why we're here so we're going to.' I picked her up with difficulty, the baby inside me kicking like a warning. We walked slowly towards the school.

'This is an adventure, darling, isn't it? Like being explorers looking for treasure. Only we're looking for a cute little deer.' Behind the school, trees shifted in a strengthening wind.

Martha clung on to me, her face in my neck. There was a muffled 'No'. I tried to put her down again so I could look at her, talk to her, but she wouldn't move. 'Martha, don't be silly. Let's go.'

I set off up the path that ran round the side of the playground and into the woods. It was narrow, bordered with nettles, and carrying Martha while navigating mud and dog shit was impossible. 'You'll have to walk,' I said and bent to put her down again. She let go this time and stood with her hands stuffed in her coat pockets, her mouth all wobbly.

'Come on, Martha,' I said again. 'Let's find the deer.'

'No.'

'Why don't you want to?'

'I'll get in trouble.' She started to cry.

'Oh, for fucks sake ...' I stopped myself. 'Sorry, sorry, sorry.' I tried to hug her, but she wouldn't let me.

A jogger ran out of the woods and down the path towards us. We both stepped back to let him pass and I was too late to stop Martha's hand catching the nettles. She yelped, then started crying even harder.

I held her hand and brushed the hair out of her eyes, all the time scanning the playground for the deer. 'It's just a nettle sting, it'll go away soon.' The playground was empty.

Martha kept crying. There was a clump of dock growing on the other side of the path and I picked a few leaves. 'Look, this'll help,' I said, rolling and crushing them until the juice came out.

She looked doubtful, but she let me press the green mush onto the sting. 'Here we go. That'll stop it hurting.'

She stared up at me, utterly miserable. 'Please can we go home?'

I gazed into the trees and then at the playground again; if I looked hard enough, if I wanted it enough, the deer would be there. Though it wasn't.

I nodded and took her other hand. We walked slowly back towards the road.

Not long afterwards I did see the deer. I was late picking Martha up from the after-school club and it was already getting dark as I crossed the playground. A square of light from one of the classrooms lay across the chippings under the play tower. As I hurried past, there was a scrabbling noise and a dark shape – not much bigger than a cat – skittered away into the shadows. I caught a glimpse of small curved antlers like speech marks over its head.

Martha was waiting at the door. The grumpy assistant waiting with her told me off for being late again and said they'd have to charge this time. 'That's OK,' I said. 'It doesn't matter.'

I didn't tell Martha about the deer. Two weeks later we had another letter from the school to say it had got caught in the fence at the back of the playground and had had to be put down.

That's years ago now. I can't remember the last time Martha held my hand. Now she's aloof, loping ahead of me on long teenage legs when she deigns to be seen with me in public. Matty's the same, copying his older sister even if he doesn't quite know why. For so long there was a small, soft hand in mine every time I left the house; it seemed it would always be that way. Sometimes I cry, remembering.

The last deer I saw was from a train, travelling north. The muddy winter landscape of the south was slowly streaked with patches of snow, more and more of it until the window filled up with white. Martha and Matty were sleeping and I thought about waking them, to show them this wonder, but I kept it for myself.

The train slowed as we passed a black fence and a clump of black trees, a black stream sliding through them and under the track. Then there was a square white field, flat as a sheet of paper. A deer was high-stepping through the snow, halfway across now, its hoof prints black marks on the page. When I glanced over, Martha was awake but fiddling with her phone, so it was just me who watched the deer, just me who stared at the message I couldn't read.

A Series of Faces

Jess Richards

After living together in a comfortable home, a faded woman and man get married. Their love turns into sadness and they kiss each other good night as an afterthought. During the daytimes, the sun deliberately pulls light away from them.

The woman imagines the fingernails of old women called witches and stares at her hands. She whispers to herself, 'I wish I'd never grown up.'

The clock strikes midnight.

The man reads a news story about an old man who's sending thousands of young men to war to die because of what he wants.

He murmurs to himself, 'What would it feel like, to have that kind of power?'

The woman is probably meant to tell him he's already powerful, but she doesn't.

They have little to say to each other besides describing how beautiful they once were.

Bliss, wedded.

The clock strikes eleven.

In an attempt to become lighter together, the couple travel away from their marital home. In a desert wilderness they disassemble their tent again and again, waiting for the stars to align and rekindle their love. But this wilderness is a place only ever meant to be walked through—to get to a happier location.

One morning, they wake up kissing.

Kissing makes the woman feel younger. It also makes her cry.

Inside their beige tent the man says, 'You're blinding me.'

'With what?' She licks one of her tears from his lip.

'Salt.'

His pupils are coal-black.

She says, 'You only look blind in the same way a tunnel is blind.'

He clenches his fist.

'I do love you,' she says. 'I do.'

The clock strikes ten.

The young woman examines the campfire's fading sparks. This wilderness isn't working any magic; it is made of sand and stone and sky.

She no longer wants to be married.

The fire blusters smoke and ignites itself. A sign that lightness and warmth might soon be coming to her.

Her husband wanders away from their tent. His arms reach, opening wider and wider.

She watches his outstretched hands, grasping.

He calls, 'Where are you?' as if he really is blind. He blunders across sand, puppet-like, distorted.

A lone actor on a desert stage.

The clock strikes nine.

Thorns blow up from the sand. He catches them and pushes them into his eyes. Blood runs as tears. Between thumb and fingertip, one remaining thorn. Outstretched. He walks slowly. 'Come here,' he speaks. Softer. 'Come to me, wife. I need you.'

She imagines she is light and he will chase and catch her, causing her to disappear. She imagines she is a shadow and he will chase and catch her, causing her to disappear. She thinks of swans chased by thunderclouds, mice chased by cats, rats chased by swans, and thunderclouds chased by dogs. She imagines chasing a fox, a badger, a hare. She imagines becoming all these creatures simultaneously.

Heart full of animal spirits, she flees him.

The clock strikes eight.

Passing blackthorn bushes and ivy-bound trees the woman steps on shuddering nettle shadows, climbs mossy walls, and wades through her own warping reflection in streams. Surrounded by bramble bushes is a stone clocktower with no door.

She has answered its call.

A glassless window gapes beneath the clock's face. A rope ladder extends down the wall as an invitation. And so, she climbs. As she eases her body over the window ledge the rope ladder dissolves like steam. A coil of gold rope appears like a snake on the floor.

A dark-haired witch looks up from a worn armchair and says, 'You're safe here. Don't leave.' The witch winds peel from a blood orange and hands it to the young woman.

The young woman splits the orange and hands half back to the witch.

They eat their segments simultaneously, counting them, eyeing each other. Checking for signs of health, for signs of trust. Checking that the blood of the orange isn't poisoned.

The clock strikes seven.

On the floorboards between the young woman and the witch, shadows shift. Big small. Small big. They glance at each other with curiosity; something not quite right, something not quite wrong.

The witch and the young woman stand side by side at a glassless window. They inhale the scents of oranges and pine trees.

The young woman tells the witch, 'I've left my husband and he needed me. Now, I know nothing I thought I knew.'

The witch replies, 'Wind blows into married minds. And rain. Sunshine breaks through cloud. Time shifts quick slow. Slow quick.'

The clock strikes six.

The witch says, 'You've heard of the number six, repeated thrice? There is no such thing as a devil. There are devilish human acts.'

The witch shows the young woman a view of kings slaying princes, of princes grabbing princesses, and princesses painting their faces on, like masks, and becoming queens.

The young woman shows the witch a view of bones in a desert wilderness.

The witch shows the young woman a view of queen bees and fruit flies, ants defending mud cities, painted butterflies and armoured beetles.

The young woman shows the witch a view of her abandoned pastel-coloured home, her husband's tight wedding band, a cravat as a bib, a wedding dress as a ghost, an empty wooden cradle; claimed by the cat. The young woman sighs and tells the witch, 'I never wanted what everyone said I should want. It was all an act.'

The clock strikes five.

On the whitewashed wall the witch's shadow, dark blue and beckoning, picks up a coil of gold rope.

The witch swipes a pair of scissors through the air around the young woman's head. The young woman's hair grows, merging and tangling around the strands of the rope.

With a scarlet hairbrush the witch and her shadow frizz the young woman's rope-hair into gold clouds and smooth it all out again. Plait and untangle, tangle and plait.

The rope-hair winds itself around the young woman's neck, gleaming.

The witch says, 'I need to go away for a while. To learn you, I have to unlearn myself.'

The clock strikes four.

Alone without the witch, there aren't enough shadows. The young woman wraps herself in her hair. The strands dance; dawn light against skin. She winds and unwinds herself, pulls and tugs, testing her strength.

Inside the witch's clocktower there is a lilac bed with no pillow, pale embroidery threads with no needle, books with multi-coloured spines and no ink. There is a purple jug of water that refills itself each night when the clouds come indoors to rest. A bowl of rotten apples become riper and harder each day.

Her rope-hair casts and gathers light, stealing something from everything.

The clock strikes three.

The witch returns, eyes shining. The teenage girl and the witch laugh as they embrace each other. Their shadows hunch along the edges of the stone room, indigo to black to burgundy to dark green.

A man yowls from outside the window.

Rooks squall and crawk in high nests.

The teenage girl's husband is crouched in the bushes. He pulls thorns from his eyes and blood runs away. He jumps and flies up the clocktower towards the window. Hands flail, gripping stone-edges.

He sees his teenage wife with the witch and their shadows.

A scream.

Crows and ravens flit past.

He flails and falls, nails breaking against stone.

The clock strikes two.

The witch growls anger like a storm.

From the ground the girl's husband shouts, 'Sing!'

The witch asks the girl, 'Have you sung for him before?'

She replies, 'He lies about everything. Beauty. Blindness. Song. I only lied about love.'

He retreats into the trees, cracking twigs.

The witch frowns as she says, 'You lied about love?'

The girl talks in a tangle, 'Everyone lies about everything. I'm half-sick of my shadows, a poetry book speaks about this—what's the title?' She grips the witch's arm, 'What *was* the title? Something about love? It was a fairytale, but it wasn't a fairy tale...'

The clock strikes one.

The girl says, 'Is each love story really about our determination to be infinite images, repeating ourselves like little mirrors?'

The witch asks again, 'You lied about love?'

The girl slumps into a chair and examines the strands of her rope-hair. After a while she says sadly, 'The whole world's only a series of faces, isn't it?'

The clock strikes midday.

The witch tells the girl, 'You're growing younger too fast. I'm not sure where this will end.'

The witch leaves the clocktower in search of a remedy for youth.

While the girl is alone, shadows thicken inside her mind.

The witch comes back with a palmful of sea salt. 'For purification from wedded bliss.' As the witch runs salt through the girl's fingertips, her uncried tears sting and fall.

When the witch hugs the girl, her shadow dances around her, heavier than feathers, lighter than the idea of a feather.

The girl flings her rope-hair from the window and watches the witch climb down.

The clock strikes one.

The witch gives a flower back to the stem of a plant, comes back to the clocktower and climbs the girl's hair. The witch climbs down again, breathes life into a dead rabbit, climbs up again. She climbs down, pours a jug of water into the stream, climbs up.

The girl wants this to be easy; she wants to be with the witch all the time.

The witch is out planting herbs in other people's gardens.

The girl hears branches cracking. The witch must be returning. She throws her rope-hair down.

A heavy tug rips hairs from her scalp.

This is not the weight of a witch, but the weight of a man.

The clock strikes two.

The girl is far too young to be married.

Her husband's face appears at the window. He grips her hair at the roots and kisses her. She inhales the violence from his lips.

He says, 'You should sing for me, then I'll love you.' He looks at her with desire, as if this is the first time he's really seen her.

Shaking, she stares at the ground. How near it is. How far.

He says 'Don't reject me.' He climbs down her rope-hair and goes away.

The forest's branches thrash this way and that, caught in some gale she can't feel.

The clock strikes three.

Night rises and soaks the sky, but the witch doesn't come back. Day falls again, days keep falling. In the clocktower, the girl's rope-hair shines. There is the constant sound of ticking. Missing the witch, she hums a mournful tune. There is the constant sound of ticking. A new feeling shifts in the air; her tune is a spell, summoning a return. There is a constant sound of ticking. Through the glassless window she watches a full moon set over the forest.

Her husband stands beneath a tree, head tilted.

He is smaller when seen from this height.

Small as a child gulping oblivion from a wine bottle.

The clock strikes four.

The girl sings about shadows and light, tangles, threads, towers, wildernesses, deserts, thorns, salt, tears.

Her husband frowns as if hearing a strange bird he's never heard before. He turns and disappears between the trees.

As if he was never there at all, he is gone.

She feels new.

Strong.

Unmarried.

The clock strikes five, six, seven.

Days fall and fall, scattering light. The girl's rope-hair attracts light, collects it, pulls brightness into itself, and shines. She misses the weight of the witch. Through too-bright, too-light days the girl sings in and out of herself, no longer knowing if she is summoning or banishing.

The clock strikes eight.

As the girl sings, her thighs narrow and her breasts shrink. She sings and sings, her feet are too small for her shoes. She sings in and out again. Crying, she calls for the witch, 'Come play with me! Don't leave me alone!' She wants the witch and the witch is not there. But witches are uncountable, uncontrollable, and free. They travel according to their own rhythms and perceptions of time.

The clock strikes nine.

The witch's breath smells of lavender as she raises the sleepy girl to her feet and makes her stand tall.

She says, 'I've invented more spells.' She teaches the girl how to forget she is married and how to forget that she cries. She teaches her how to forget to miss anyone.

The witch goes away. She comes back and she goes away again. The witch comes back and teaches the young girl how to forget everything she's been told she should be, everything she's been told she is, and everything she's been told she should do.

The young girl says, 'There are shadows I need to forget.'

The witch says, 'Me too.'

The clock strikes ten.

The Witch's List of Ten Shadows:
The shadows of being a loving spouse.
The shadows of unsatisfied lovers.
The shadows of never-born children.
The shadows of not being wise enough.
The shadows of homelessness and hunger.
The shadows of being needed or wanted.
The shadows of beauty and ugliness.
The shadows of sexual violence.
The shadows of success or failure.
The shadows of lost power and lost hope and lost love.

The clock strikes eleven.

The Girl's List of Eleven Shadows:
The shadows of false friends and real enemies.
The shadows of not liking anyone very much, but wanting to be liked.
The shadows of doing badly what everyone else is doing well.
The shadows of broken plates, glasses, mugs, bowls, homes.
The shadows of being unheard.
The shadows of missing out on everything brilliant other people are shouting about.
The shadows of not being bright or pretty or kind enough.
The shadows of dead animals and dead plants and dead trees.
The shadows of being afraid of strangers and war and leggy insects.
The shadows of being hungry and unloved.
The shadows of marriage as a fairy tale.

The clock strikes midnight again.

The witch becomes wiser as she remembers.
The girl becomes younger as she forgets.
The witch murmurs, 'Why do we teach children anything, when they already know all they need to know? This one saw what was coming and never wanted to grow up.'
Inside the clocktower, the witch cradles a shining toddler with short golden curls.
She rocks her and rocks her till the toddler forgets language and shrinks to the size of a baby.
Pacing to and fro, the witch clutches the baby to her heart.

The clock stops.

Crawks and squalls and chirps fill the tallest treetops while dusk falls. Light floods from the clocktower window.

The shadow of a witch dances with a glowing baby.

The witch says, 'I've never wanted to have a baby of my own, until now.'

Though the baby believes this is a lie, she doesn't care.

She is already anticipating the warmth of the witch's womb, and her own conception.

Snowdrops

Rachel Burns

In the garden she noticed the stooped white heads of snowdrops. The crocuses starting to come up through the loose soil poked their purple buds, testing the air. There was something wonderful about early spring flowers. Year upon year; it always surprised her.

Earlier, she heard a woman scream, somewhere on the housing estate. The sound found her on her walk, a real visceral cry of despair, and it haunted her. She'd once screamed like that, when she'd found him in a crumpled heap, collapsed at the bottom of the stairs, the telephone table knocked sideways.

It could be something or nothing—hysteria, she reasoned with herself. Some women, she thought, are hysterical all the time for no good reason. Her grandmother had been a formidable woman who had terrible rages over spilt milk or burnt toast, or even an article in the newspaper. Her grandfather used to try to make light of it. 'Hormones,' he would say, as he ducked a flying plate.

Strange then, irrational even, that she kept her ears pricked for the sound of a siren as she walked with a purposeful stride across the farmer's muddy field. Her Wellington boots squelched in a satisfying way. She was careful to hold her breath as she went past the sewage yard, the pungency of raw effluent so powerful it made her nauseous. The physical act of holding her breath brought back memories of Jack: his constant wheezing, the strange sound he'd made like a worn-out hymn.

The path was difficult to negotiate because of all the rain, which had been relentless for months, and she was tired of mud splattering her clothes, and not being able to walk at a faster pace. She thought back to the scream; it reminded her of a line from a Sylvia Plath poem, something about a woman in an ambulance and a red heart. But there were no sirens, there was no ambulance rushing to an emergency, and she reprimanded herself in the loud stern voice her mother would have used, 'Really, Susan, you *are* silly, what fanciful ideas you have.'

Her dog was running wild in the woods somewhere; she heard the odd startled rasping sound of a pheasant flushed from its hiding place, followed by an eerie silence. The dog seemed to disappear completely. She listened to the elms, their branches creaking in the wind, diseased trunks knocking against each other. Her stomach knotted; she was a woman wholly alone in the woods.

When the two of them appeared, she was startled, her heart bouncing in her chest. A man in a red beanie hat was walking with a young boy, who she guessed was about eight, a slight, skinny child. Then her dog reappeared, running about them like a jack-in-the-box, weaving in and out of their legs like a thing possessed. Cross, she called the dog to heel and shouted an apology to the man and his boy. She presumed it was his boy; she wondered what they were doing in the woods. Shouldn't the boy be in school? Perhaps he was sick. He didn't look sick—pasty, yes, but not sick enough to warrant a day off.

The dog was deliberately ignoring her commands, still running between the boy's legs, then jumping up at the man as if expecting a treat. At last, she was able to snatch the dog by the collar, and the man said to the boy as they both passed, 'Boy, he's excitable.'

The boy, laughing, said, 'Yes.'

She relaxed then—obviously just a father and his son taking a stroll through the woods.

She remembered being with her grandfather when she was a girl, and the bluebells. Gosh, yes, the bluebells, armfuls to take back to her grandmother, and the smell of wild garlic as she knelt to pick the flowers.

Her grandfather worshipped the outdoors. 'Anyone would,' he often said, 'after years spent on hands and knees, crawling along coal seams in the dark.' He had been a miner after leaving school at fifteen, then suddenly the mines were all gone.

They would play Pooh sticks in the beck, stopping at the little bridges that crossed the railway line. He would tell her about the steam trains, about how when he was a boy, his mother used to send him down to collect the black lumps that fell off the backs of coal wagons.

She would have visions of her grandfather as a small boy on the tracks with a steam train hurtling towards him. 'Wasn't that dangerous?' she'd ask.

His eyes would gleam, and he would reply, 'Very dangerous, yes.'

He could make bows and arrows out of branches and sharpen the ends with a knife. She remembered he always had a piece of wood in his hands; he was forever whittling something, strangely shaped little animals, and mythical creatures.

Another trick he showed from time to time was to pick a handful of nettles and crunch them in his bare hands. He was immune to stings and would recount a story about how his father had kept beehives: one day, when he was only small, he was attacked by the whole hive and very nearly died.

Sometimes she forgot her grandfather was no longer alive.

There was something about the man and the boy, the way they carried themselves, the long sticks they used as walking poles. The man looked like he was making a real effort, perhaps showing the boy his childhood, perhaps saying, *These are the woods I played in as a boy.*

She was back to the sewage yard, the work van was parked up, and she thought perhaps this area was not as isolated as one might think—deceptively so, even. Plenty of people came and went, plenty of people on mobile phones. Then, once again, she was crossing the backs of the houses where she'd heard the terrible scream. There was no sound of anything untoward. *Hysteria, then*, she thought. *Nothing more.*

* * *

Later, in the quiet of the afternoon, she listened to a news programme on the local radio station and argued with the guest speaker even though he couldn't hear her. 'What a ridiculous thing to say. How would you know? You're not even married.'

Next, she aired out the bedrooms, straightening the beds, even the ones that hadn't been slept in for years, opening the windows, letting in the fresh air. She spotted black mildew growing around the window in Junior's room and made a mental note to bleach it. Later, she knew, she would put it off for weeks because she hated the powerful smell of ammonia. It reminded her too much of hospitals.

Then she did the day's washing-up; she liked to leave her breakfast and dinner plates in the sink to soak and do the whole lot after supper. She had allowed herself to do this for some time, grown accustomed to the mess malaudering in the sink. She had picked 'malaudering' up from her mother; she didn't even think it is a real word.

When the washing-up was done, dried and put away, she sat in the kitchen chair watching the sky gradually darken. The radio presenter talked about the day's events, the same old headlines of police corruption and budget cuts. She found she was listening more intently than usual.

She didn't know why she thought there might be a terrible announcement: a missing boy, a stabbing, a bloodstained knife. Then her mind wandered off, and she imagined she was walking through the woods again, this time accompanied by a nice young policeman about her son's age. She was showing him exactly where she saw the young boy strolling with that man. Oh yes, she could describe him very accurately: mid-twenties, a red beanie hat, medium build, brown hair, brown eyes. 'That is what struck me,' she said, 'the eyes. They were frantic eyes, those of someone running scared.'

* * *

She's been lost in thought for some time when her mobile phone rings—the Shostakovich tune, the one that everyone knows. Junior downloaded it for her when he purchased the phone. She hadn't the heart to tell him how much she hated Shostakovich; it was music that belonged to Jack Senior, not her.

'Hello, Mum.'

'Oh, Jack Junior, it's you.' Her son always rings on Tuesday evenings at seven o'clock. He worries if she doesn't answer. She looks out of the window, surprised to see that it is dark already.

'Please don't call me that, Mum. You okay?'

'Oh dear,' she glances at the kitchen clock, 'is that the time already?' She suddenly feels very tired.

'Sorry, Mum, is it a bad time? Do you want me to ring back later?'

'No, no, Jack, it's lovely to hear your voice, you know what I'm like. I was away with the fairies.'

They laugh together, a little conspiratorial laugh.

When Jack Senior was alive, he used to get so cross. She remembers that he used to think they were laughing at him. It was as if he was jealous that she and Jack Junior had something between them that he couldn't quite grasp.

She tells Jack Junior about her day, about the blood-curdling scream and the strange man (for now in her imagination he has grown strange) with the little boy who should have been in school.

'It's probably nothing, Mum.'

His voice reassures her; he is right, of course. She spends far too much time on her own, letting her imagination run away with her.

* * *

She opened the patio doors and let the dog out into the garden; it was a clear night, and she could see the stars, the waxing gibbous moon. She remembered nights like this when Jack Senior was in the hospital, all those clear nights when she gazed out of the window from Ward 23, marvelling at the night sky and listening to her husband struggle to breathe, to the sound of the oxygen machine and to the magnified ticking of the clock.

She remembered the harassed social worker who talked to her at the hospital. 'Being a full-time carer isn't easy.'

If only she knew. Jack Senior's temper had got worse as

his shortness of breath slowly deteriorated, eventually reaching the point where he couldn't even manage the stairs. But he was adamant he was not going to sleep on the sofa bed downstairs.

She watched him, stubborn as a mule, climbing to the top, clean out of breath, his face turning blue. 'Help me, Woman.' He could barely get the words out; she could barely hear him.

She should have gone to help him, at least fetched the nebuliser, but she just stood there and watched. She was worn out with it all, the constant call to duty. She was looking forward to taking the dog for a walk in the fresh air. Thirty minutes of peace, away from him. It was a shock when he fell, his body crashing down the stairs, his head hitting the telephone table, knocking it sideways. He lay at the bottom of the stairs, not moving. She was stunned into silence.

Then there was the scream, that terrible scream, that came from deep inside her.

At first she was terrified he was dead, but then something kicked in, and she was checking his pulse, faint but still there. In slow motion she picked up the telephone stand, then the telephone, placed it back on the table and dialled 999.

'Ambulance, please.' Her voice was detached, as calm as anything.

There was a great deal of blood where he had bashed his head. Her heart thumped so hard, she could feel it in her rib cage, yet she managed to find a clean tea towel. She sat and cradled his head as they waited for the ambulance to arrive, the blood seeping into the white cloth like a rose in bloom. He lost consciousness and came around only fleetingly; she'd never forgotten the look in his eyes.

A few days in the hospital, a machine to help him breathe,

then the decision not to revive. Jack Junior said it was the right thing to do.

She let the dog back into the house from the garden, locked the doors and made her way upstairs to bed. She closed the sash-window, cleaned her teeth at the little sink, undressed, put on her nightie and climbed into her side of the bed. She loved this time of the evening, the smell and feel of cool aired sheets against her skin. With the clear night sky imprinted on her brain, she drifted off into a deep sleep.

Unseen

Kathryn Aldridge-Morris

Your abdomen is lined with keyholes like a motel corridor, each leading to a plum-red room, plush and bloody. No lover has entered these rooms; only this man in pistachio scrubs, his laparoscope probing your foliage with metal antennae, finding your twenties writ large like hieroglyphs the length of your liver, then your thirties' postpartum depressed—congealed into fossilised balls of fat. He journeyed your flesh. Mapped your organs. And now, in cufflinks and suit, his fingers press on your epigastrium. When he asks how you've been this past month, you don't tell him you've googled post-op risks and the symptoms of those risks; how one in ten, a hundred, a thousand mean nothing; how your mother died of a one in sixty thousand chance cancer, how your father's was three in a million. You don't mention the abrading anxiety of bile leaks, endoscopies, and duct damage, of further surgery, found cancer, of the fears which fester behind more dark keyholes. You take in his perfect Italian suit, smile and say fine. Then he says, tenderly now, I'm going to undress your wounds. You lie back and he remarks how beautiful they look, and you ask, Really?

They do. These surface wounds. So neat. Once he's finished the undressing, he says call him, if you need, shifts his glasses onto his thick head of hair, says the wounds will disappear in no time. You understand. There will be nothing left to see. There never is.

Cold Salt Water

Maria C. McCarthy

He comes in with his shirt splattered with blood, and I say, 'Honest to God, Kieran.'

'Don't fuss, Mum,' he says like it's nothing to walk in the house with your nose spread across your face.

'What in Jesus' name happened?' No answer. 'Who were you with?'

'John and Chris.'

'And are they hurt too?'

'Leave it, Mum.'

I put my hand up to his face, but he dips from it. 'It's a rough old place, that dancehall. Tiffany's was it?'

'It's a disco, Mum, not a dancehall.'

And then his father's in the doorway, and I say, 'Will you look at the state of Kieran?' But he's three sheets to the wind himself, so I send him off to bed.

Well, I try to whip the shirt off the boy, but he holds it close around him. So I get a bucket ready; cold water with a good dash of salt. 'Come on now, Kieran,' I say, 'Let's have that shirt.' It's one of his good ones, a Ben Sherman. He unbuttons it. There are bruises like footprints on his chest.

'Did you get a look at them? Could you describe them to the police?'

'Please, Mum. It doesn't matter.'

'You've bruises all over!'

He flinches as I touch him. I can see that he's trying to hold on to the tears. I know the wobble in that lip, like when his father used to tell him that boys don't cry, so he'd sniff the snot back up into his nose, and pretend he was all right. But a mother knows. But a mother only knows by rummaging in his chest of drawers when he's out, through the piles of pennies and silver in the top drawer from his turned out pockets. I go in there when I'm short of money for the milkman, or need a 50p when the electric's gone. He doesn't like the rattle of the coins in his pockets, and how they spoil the line of his trousers. So they pyramid higher in the drawer, silver on copper, and slip like the coal in the bunker as the drawer opens, heavier each time I pull it out. And that's where I found that thing once – a rubber johnny, from a packet of three, and only the one left. I told him what Fr Westland would say. He just laughed. Though there have been times when I've thought, wouldn't we have been glad of one of those?

He's been worse since he's been working, acting like he's man of the house. Home at six, he slams the back door open against the kitchen dresser – there's a hole in the hardboard now – then he shouts, 'Where's my dinner?' When he was small, I could slap him across the back of the legs, but now he stands above me. I need to stand on a chair to look him in the eye.

'I'm off to bed,' Kieran says. I watch as he climbs the stairs, every step an effort. Whether he sleeps or not, I don't know, but I lie awake next to his snoring father. Every time I close my eyes, I can't stop seeing the footprints on my boy's chest.

In the morning, he's so stiff he can hardly raise an arm, so I knock at Mick Bennett's house, and ask would he tell them at the factory that Kieran won't be in. Then I run Kieran a hot bath to see if it would ease him a little, and make him egg and bacon once he is out, and dressed. Although it hurts to see him like that, it's nice, in a way, to have my boy to myself, with Jack and the children off for the day.

I've the radio on in the kitchen, and the news headlines come over, of the latest from the IRA, a pub in Guildford, not ten miles up the road. I know there'll be hard stares when I ask for the veg at the greengrocer, when I open my mouth to speak, as if it was me that laid that bomb. 'Are you ready to tell me?' I say, as he wipes the yolk of his egg off the plate with a half-bitten slice of fried bread. He holds up his mug, and I pour some more tea. 'Shall we go to the police?' He half-drains the mug, then slams it down on the table. The tea splashes up the sides then settles again. 'Or was it you that started it? I know your temper.'

The full story of the bombing comes on the radio. 'Switch it off,' he says.

'God knows why your father stands up for that lot,' I say, 'it doesn't do us any good, those of us that have to live here.' He stares at his plate, his fingertips pressing into the edge of the table. 'Is that what the fight was over?' I say.

'It's nothing to do with me, what the Irish get up to,' he says, 'I ain't Irish.'

I wipe my hands on a tea towel and turn to him. 'Only every ounce of blood that flows through your veins.'

'It don't make me Irish.' He butters a slice of bread. I can see how it's bothering him to eat, with his top lip split. Part of me wants to slap him, and the rest of me wants to cradle him. I picture him lying on the ground as the heavy boots hit his chest. And I think of how he's stopped going to the Tara club, how it's Tiffany's on a Saturday night,

43

out with his packet of three: Durex, approved to British standards.

I go to the bucket where I'd steeped his shirt the night before. The water is pink, blood seeping into the crystals. I drain the bucket into the sink, rinse the shirt, then run more cold water into the bucket, emptying in the remainder of the packet of Saxa. I watch the shirt sink, pushing it down so it's covered.

My Mother's Twelfth Suitor

Reshma Ruia

For her eightieth birthday, I buy my mother a red wheelchair. She chooses the model from a catalogue called Pride Mobility and is won over when the small print says the wheels are assembled in England not China and are made out of a nylon/fibreglass-like material that is strong, resilient and lightweight, designed to withstand the British rain. 'That does it,' she says. 'It's British. It won't let me down.'

'It's better than Dad's. More nimble.' I jerk my chin towards my father's ungainly black wheelchair parked in front of the lounge window, where it sits, like a large toad blocking out the light.

Slowly, insidiously my parents have begun competing with each other, collecting accoutrements of old age like Brownie badges. Dentures, walking sticks, folding stools, Zimmer frames, even the occasional commode. They graduate from one to the other with the glee of a child learning to walk and talk again.

'Your father's wheelchair looks like it was made in the Soviet Union and we all know what happened to that country.' Mother raises an eyebrow and tut tuts while my father chuckles and says all he's interested in is getting from A to B and some days even A to A minus will do.

My mother has arthritic knees. Her red wheelchair is an aeroplane in which I whizz her in and out of doctors' rooms

45

and x-ray labs, Indian grocery stores and parking lots. Today I'm driving her across town to see an orthopaedist who can help to halt the sound of her bones grinding to ash. Mother sits next to me, round like a knitting ball. Bright lipsticked mouth and forehead smeared with Tiger balm.

We're talking about marriages and husbands. She's speaking about my father without saying his name.

'Highly overrated, this marriage business. Don't be in a rush to jump in.' She pats the brown handbag on her lap like a pet cat.

'Why did you get married then?' I challenge her. It's a stupid question really. She is eighty and has been married for almost sixty years. This is no time for new reckonings.

She leans forward, fiddling with the knobs on the dashboard and raises the heating up a notch, until the air inside the car is a fug of stale warmth.

'It's 22 degrees, Ma. It's June for heaven's sake.' I wind down the window and then roll it up again, remembering her age. She is old and needs light and heat to preserve her fragility.

There is silence. My mother is thinking.

'I had twelve suitors,' she announces at the traffic lights. 'One committed suicide and ten stayed unmarried, but there was one who got away. He was the one I fancied.'

Car horns honk as traffic lights turn from red to green but I stay still, my foot like a stone on the brake pad.

'You're kidding?' I stare at her, my mouth open, seeing her through the twelve suitors' eyes. I imagine her svelte hipped with dimpled cheeks and long lashed eyes.

'His name was Bansal. My aunt was his mother's best friend. She showed us his photo one day and we were all smitten. He was tall. He smoked cigars and wrote Persian poetry on weekends.'

'He sounds too good to be true, a bit of a dandy really,' I say, defending my dad whose favourite pastime was eating Margherita pizza and watching reruns of *Dallas* on daytime TV.

She nods. 'He was one of a kind.'

We arrive at the hospital. Dr Cranston, the orthopaedist, has American teeth – white pearls strung along his baby pink gums and a mop of sandy hair he keeps pushing back with a languid hand. In another life, he might have been a cruise ship crooner belting out Frank Sinatra. But for now he must pass his days tending to the knees of geriatric patients who have been careless in their youth. He scrunches up his eyes, bringing up the image of my mother's knees on the screen. The ravaged bones shine through.

'You've left it too late,' he says, shaking his head.

'What about cortisone injections?' I pipe up.

He waves this away. His gaze floats back to the x-ray where my mother's damaged knees glint like a murder weapon.

'Can you see the cartilage there?'

I nod at the ivory-coloured blurred shadow on the screen.

'There are several alternatives one could consider but given her age...' he says. 'I could do an arthroscopic washout and debridement or an osteotomy.'

'Stop.' Mother cuts him mid-sentence. 'I'll just have to live with these buggers that's that. Nothing doing. Just prescribe me some more painkillers.' And with that my mother hauls herself into her wheelchair and taps the arm rest with one red painted fingernail ready for take-off.

We drive home.

'What about this Bansal. The suitor who got away eh. Did he even exist or have you made him up?' I want to lighten the mood, make her feel good about life again.

'Oh, he existed all right. The wedding date was set. I

was all giddy with delight.' She smiles and squeezes my arm.

'I was only nineteen remember. People got married young those days. It was the quickest and most legal way of having sex and I couldn't wait.'

She giggles, pats her knees and says, 'It's good to talk of icebergs.'

'Icebergs? What do you mean?' My mother's mind is going the same way as her knees, I think.

'It's simple really,' she explains. 'We get older and little parts of ourselves fall away, like icebergs floating out of view and suddenly when you think all is lost, you turn a corner and there it is, that little blob of ice you thought you'd never see again. But it is there all along, you just got busy doing other things and didn't see it. That's how it is with Bansal. He's that little blob that I've just remembered to remember.'

This moment may never come back.

I think of Dad, who has spent his life filling dental cavities, and writing seminar papers on genetics and oral health.

'Well, Bansal's loss is Dad's gain. You're so happy together.'

I keep my tone light and bright and turn on the radio where Louis Armstrong is singing about a wonderful world.

'Your father is a good man. He is reliable like a cargo ship but that Bansal he was something else. He was a Ferrari speedboat.' She narrows her eyes and stares out of the car window.

'So what happened to this speedboat? Why did he leave you on the shore? How come he didn't want to be with you?' I am being cruel about her bubble-gum pink memories.

'Want is such a big and scary word, isn't it?' She smiles and carries on.

'I met Bansal a week before the wedding. He came to see me in the park next to my house. We walked for a bit. It was a cool late spring evening. The gulmohur trees were bursting with flowers. I wore my favourite cream chiffon sari. We strolled in silence, admiring the roses and the dahlias. He led me to a bench near the pond and we threw peanuts at the ducks. I was so worried about getting my sari dirty, sitting on that dusty bench. At some point, Bansal took hold of my hand and told me to stop shaking. I was that nervous. I was thinking, any minute now, he is going to kiss me.' My mother stopped and looked at me. 'Can you imagine it – me a nervous, little trembly thing!'

'When did Dad appear?' I ask, suddenly impatient with her memories. I want to drag her back to the present.

She raises her hand, 'Let me finish. He kept holding my hand and recited some words from Rumi.' Her eyes go dreamy. *'The wound is the place where the Light enters you.'* That is what he said. I thought he was being romantic, but he was only preparing me for heartbreak.'

'I'm surprised he didn't read you any of his Persian poetry, it was probably just rubbish,' I say, pulling into my mother's driveway. I stop the car but my mother makes no attempt to get out and stays sitting. She is there but she is no longer with me. She is watching herself on that bench, smoothing the pleats of her favourite sari, her heart like a sparrow beating its wings, her damp, sweaty hand clasped by a man whose breath smells of Cuban cigars.

'Are you okay, mother?' I nudge her back to today.

'Bansal called off the wedding.' Her voice lowers. 'He told me he was moving to Australia, to set up home with another man. I didn't understand him at first. What did he mean when he said he was in love with a man and it was his parents who were forcing him into marriage with me? How could I not be good enough for him? I got up and ran back home, sobbing all the way. I never wore that sari again. It was such a scandal. We had to tell the relatives and I cried and refused to go to college. Bansal wrote to my parents explaining how he didn't want to ruin my life.' There is a faint tremor in her voice. He said, 'I don't have the right mindset for your daughter. Just imagine what a waste of a life.' She sighs loudly, as though expelling a deep load from somewhere inside her.

'As for your Dad.' Her stare is cold and cruel like a stranger's. 'You've got your mousy limp hair from him... that's for sure; anyway, I met your Dad six months later. He'd come to my university to do some research. I often saw him in the library. He had a thermos of tea and he used to drink it with noisy slurps. The librarian was always ticking him off. He was so studious, his nose buried in books. I don't think he even noticed me. It was monsoon time; I was waiting at the bus stop one day getting soaked to the skin. He drove past in a second-hand Morris Minor, saw me, reversed and offered me a lift. The next day he turned up at the bus stop again, ready to drive me home. My mother liked him, I remember him examining her mouth for cavities and giving away free Binaca toothpaste to my cousins. That was that. I ended up becoming a dentist's wife.'

That night I dream of my mother and Bansal slow waltzing in the Australian outback. Her knees are round, soft and shiny like a child's. His arm is around her waist. Above them is the sky, drunk with a thousand stars.

Women's Work

Cath Barton

June 1st, 1500

Dear Mother

Every day I rise at 4am because there is bread to put upon the table here in The Garden and I am one of those who make it. We mix and knead the dough and while it is rising we have time to ourselves. Time to write as I am doing now. I am eager to tell you of my new life.

The other women here are companionable. We work together and we all work hard. When I place my loaves with their crisp golden crusts upon the table I feel pleased and proud of myself. I am just a little sad that the men consume the bread so quickly and without recognition that we have toiled to make it. They act as if it has dropped from heaven. What do they know? None of them rise from their beds and come into The Garden before the sun has risen so high in the sky that you can no longer see the spiders' webs in the bushes or the footprints of the small birds in the damp earth. It is their loss, but still, to me, a pity; I could wish things were otherwise. Please do not think me discontent, though, quite the opposite. I have my own bed, I do not go hungry and there is sweet birdsong in my ears every morning.

I beg you to take no notice of any unpleasant rumours which reach your ears about The Garden. I know they are out there, but they are a gross distortion of the truth, spread by people who are jealous.

Your obedient daughter

Marcia

There follow, here and after subsequent letters, extracts from an account of the findings of the annual review of the pleasure garden named 'Of Earthly Delights', hereafter referred to as 'The Garden', for the 12 month period ending December 1500. Records of the pleasure gardens of Brabant go back to 1441, since when an annual review has been conducted by representatives of the regional administrative body. The Garden has always received high commendation and is held up as a model of excellence throughout the region.

From the Brabant Archives, Inspection of pleasure gardens, 1500

3a) There are in The Garden five women bakers, who each day bake one hundred loaves and, sometimes, sweet fancies. The ovens are clean and the baked goods need no special protection from flies and vermin as they are quickly consumed. The position of baker is passed from woman to woman as they wish. On average women undertake the role for between four and six months. The system appears to function satisfactorily. The workers report no discontent.

Recommendation: That the bakery operation continue unchanged.

Dearest Mother

I received your letter this morning with delight which turned to melancholy when I read your sombre words. Let me try to set your mind at rest by telling you a little more about the lives of the women here.

We have in The Garden a system of bathing pools, fed by spring water which rises in the blue hills to the north. Each morning, as I walk to my work in the kitchens, I delight to see the water sparkling and the birds flying to and fro over my head singing to the glory of God.

The pools are central to the diversions offered to the men who visit each day, who are many. That water is fresh and clean, but in the pools is daily sullied by the bodies of those who bathe. So, in the evening hours, when the men have left The Garden, there are women who sweep fine nets through the pools, gathering and fishing out all that should not be there.

All the women who bathe in the pools with the men take a turn at helping with the cleaning. I look forward to the day when I will take on that job. It is an important one, contributing to harmony and peace. When people speak to you of licentiousness, dearest Mother, remember that I am here and they are not. There is always another side to the story.

Your ever-loving daughter
Marcia

From the Brabant Archives, Inspection of pleasure gardens, 1500 (Extracts, continued)

5a) The system for keeping the water in the pools clean depends on the voluntary cooperation of all the women employed in service of the men. The waste matter which the women clear daily from the pool is spread under the fruit bushes of The Garden, where it appears to provide them with nourishment. The fruit crops in The Garden are of a remarkable abundance. However, the practice of allowing the birds of The Garden to bathe in the pools alongside the men and women is unsanitary.

Recommendations: That the system for cleaning the pools be formalised; and

That birds be kept away from the bathing pools at all times.

September 1st, 1500

Dear Mother

I am sorry that you feel angry. I have hesitated about writing to you again, but it is a new month and I have made a resolution; there is nothing to be gained by my silence.

You expressed special concern about the mess made by the birds. Perhaps I can paint a better picture for you. There are women whose job is to feed the birds. We have many different species living in The Garden, some far from their natural habitats. Birds of forest, savannah and field boundaries live together here. The bird-feeders attend to their individual needs, whether they be for nuts and seeds, fruits or small mammals. We cannot have rodents running free amongst the people, so we have a system of tunnels through which they may move freely – we abhor cruelty – but from which we can pluck them when needed. At night, when the men have left The Garden, we open the hatches so that the creatures can run free; the owls can then swoop and pick up their own prey. We aim for a balance. It is not a perfect system but show me a better one.

I do hope this helps to allay your fears.
Your daughter
Marcia

From the Brabant Archives, Inspection of pleasure gardens, 1500 (Extracts, continued)
    5b) There were no vermin observed running free in The Garden. The system in place for ensuring that any rats are caught by raptors is an excellent one.
    Recommendation: That pest control systems continue unchanged.

October 10th, 1500

Mother
I beg you to remember that without work there is no money. I am sorry to speak frankly but I cannot let the allegations which you made in your last letter go unchallenged. You are repeating the words of ignorant people.
    Yes, it is true that those women who have no specialist job renounce their individual names while they are working in The Garden. And yes, we all wear our hair long and are expected to adopt the same attitude of blank compliance when we attend to the desires of the men. But, I repeat, we are working women, and this is a much more pleasant environment in which to work than the fish market or one of the taverns in the market square. Here we are in the open air, and there is no marauding. And if men do not follow the rules they are expelled from The Garden.
    Marcia

From the Brabant Archives, Inspection of pleasure gardens, 1500 (Extracts, continued)

7) There are one hundred women employed in The Garden, servicing, on average, three hundred men each day. Vacancies in The Garden arise only rarely; there is currently a long waiting list. Job opportunities for women are very restricted throughout the province of Brabant. On the day the inspection was carried out The Garden was full to capacity. Comments made to us suggest that there is a level of unmet need in the town.

Recommendation: That consideration be given to expansion of The Garden towards the north.

November 5th, 1500

Dear Mother

I am sorry that you felt I was abrupt in my last letter. It is never my wish to upset you, please remember that.

And I have good news! I have moved from the bakery to a job in administration, one of a small team of women. We make sure that all the systems here in The Garden work smoothly – the timings for the pool circuits, the clearing of the rotting fruit and distribution of the fresh, and so on. The Queen of The Garden invites us to meet with her weekly, and if any of us have ideas for improvements we are encouraged to put them forward to her. It is good to share ideas. I like this work. It makes me feel that I matter.

I do not have time to write more just now, today we have a firework display to prepare, but be assured, all is well here as I trust it is with you.

Your loving daughter
Marcia

From the Brabant Archives, Inspection of pleasure gardens, 1500 (Extracts, continued)

10) The administrative systems in The Garden were

established by the founder. They are comprehensive and fully documented and a copy is kept off-site. During our visit we observed all these systems to be running smoothly.

Recommendation: That administrative systems continue unchanged.

December 2nd, 1500

Dear Mother

I feel sure that I have told you about the Queen of the Garden before, but if you say not, I am sorry.

Put simply, she is the person in charge. Yes, we *do* have a woman in charge, why would we not? There is no commandment that men should determine everything in this world, is there? Does it say that in the Bible? And, tell me this, is not Mary the Queen of Heaven?

You ask what there is for her to do, when we have 'all these fancy systems' as you put it. Yes, we do have systems, as I described in my last letter, but you know, Mother, we are only human here and the men seem to want things both ways. They do not want to hear our opinions, but when we just go along with what they ask they are not happy with that either. It is difficult to know how to respond and that is where the Queen comes in – we can go to her at any time. We can talk to her, woman to woman. And she listens.

Now do you understand?

With love, always

Marcia

From the Brabant Archives, Inspection of pleasure gardens, 1500 (Extracts, continued)

11) The Queen of the Garden is elected for a term of three years. Her role is to maintain the status quo. Applicants must have previously worked as either baker, pool cleaner or bird feeder for a minimum of one year. All the women in The Garden have a single transferable vote in elections. Members of the inspection team were approached by several people with complaints about the current Queen exceeding her remit.

Recommendation: That an investigation be set up into the actions of the Queen of the Garden over the past year, and a report be brought to the regional body within six months of the date of this report.

January 1st, 1501

Dear Mother

I'm wondering why I have not heard from you, but no doubt you are tired after all the demands of the festive season. I hope this new year finds you well and that you enjoyed the gifts I sent for Christmas. The sweet oranges came from our greenhouses.

The year has started quietly here in The Garden, but I am sure that things will change. They always do, do they not? There is a rumour of some kind of investigation into the way things run here. Some of our customers are unhappy, it seems. Well, let them go elsewhere, I say. This is not the only pleasure garden in Brabant.

With love
Marcia

February 14th, 1501

Mother

So once again you are angry with me. I fear you do not like me speaking my mind. I am sorry, but I am as entitled to my opinion as anyone else, man or woman.

Perhaps we should not write to one another for a while.

Marcia

May 2nd, 1501

Dear Mother

Thank you for holding out an olive branch. I am sorry. I truly am. I do not want to cut off contact.

Things are changing here. A large group of men left The Garden recently, travelling south, so people say. Good luck to them. We have the space we need to take in new customers. There is talk of expanding The Garden. It was recommended in a report after an inspection last year, apparently. I do remember men who were not like our usual customers. Ha! So they were officials. Well, they certainly benefitted fully from all that is on offer here for the gratification of men.

Apparently they dared to criticise the Queen of The Garden. They had received complaints. That must be what the rumoured investigation was all about. But apparently the Queen refused to give them access. Good for her, I say.

I am so glad to have your support, Mother. We women must stand together. Now and always.

Your ever-loving daughter

Marcia

From the Brabant Archives, Inspection of pleasure gardens, 1500, Addendum, 2016
There is no report on record of the investigation referred to in section 11) above and it is not known whether it was carried out. Furthermore there are no Inspection of pleasure gardens reports in the Brabant Archive with more recent dates than 1500. Other sources suggest that by c.1600

intimate relations between men and women in the pleasure gardens of the region had ceased, and that all the gardens had reverted to horticultural use only. The cultivation of tulips for the international market dates from this period. Aerial photography shows the outlines of the mediaeval pleasure gardens on the tulip fields of today, although the exact location of the garden named 'Of Earthly Delights' is not known.

My father is a good man

Kate Vine

We buried my father on a Tuesday.

Though the sun had gone down, the air remained warm; I remember my mother suddenly sweating – her skin one moment dry, the next slick. Poppy shivered and I shifted from foot to foot, unsure where to land. The smell of nearby calla lilies moved back and forth, waves of acid and jasmine.

They matter, I think.

The details.

I still count them before I go to sleep, make sure I remember each one. I colour them in, going up to but never outside the lines.

*

My father was a good man.

This phrase echoed throughout my childhood, parroted by friends and neighbours, Father Henry. It wedged itself in my ears, the most stubborn of wax, and that's how it was for me, something uncomfortable to be dug out and discarded, if only

I had the strength.

Though it clung, however, it could never infiltrate, be felt as truth. I tried; I always wanted to believe what others did, I found comfort in consensus.

A follower, my mother called me.

But I could never believe this, despite my effort. Growing up, the phrase made me sick –

sick at school, into my lunch box; emptied into the alley on our walk home, Poppy keeping watch –

sick at swim class, down the drain in the changing rooms, stomach juices joining chlorinated dirt as it slid down one hole or another –

sick at home, into a sock, which I hid under my bed until the house fell silent and then flung from the window into the garden next door.

I've since wondered what they thought, our neighbours, finding socks filled with vomit amongst their treasured raspberry plants. But they were quiet people, I understood this, even then, with no taste for the weird or unaccounted for.

I'm sure those socks were never spoken of.

*

The day after the burial, Poppy and I sat on the wall at the bottom of the garden, swinging our legs like we did when we were kids. The fields stretched out for miles, broken only by frail fences, sporadic trees, a stream I could just glimpse on the horizon. We used to have a game, Poppy and I, to see who dared run the furthest from the house; once I got as far as this grand oak tree and Poppy looked at me with such reverence. But one day my father caught us, and we never ventured past the wall again – never dared even think of it.

Poppy's calf occasionally brushed mine and we listed the things we could smell. Manure, above all. The cows found this field particularly attractive for relieving themselves; I often wondered if they were expressing disdain. Poppy swore she could smell the Japanese anemones my mother had cultivated in her flowerbeds, their bright pinks and mauves shaking in the sun. I told her they had no scent, that they don't produce nectar, but Poppy didn't care for my facts, she never had.

She wore a plain linen dress that day. She didn't dislike embellishment, I just doubt it occurred to her. The new curve of her stomach was softly visible beneath the fabric, to me at least, once I knew to look for it. She seemed so detached, I couldn't imagine her in childbirth, screaming, wrenched inside out. I wondered if I should consider the baby itself an embellishment, to her life, to ours; or

an imposter, perhaps, or

a harbinger.

Occasionally her fingers touched the very surface of her belly, but it was unclear if she was aware of this movement. To me, she was a woodland stick, dropped into the river and taken by its current. I could only watch from the bridge for her to come out the other side.

*

I used to ask my mother: what does it mean, I said, that my father is a good man?

I was nine the first time I asked; only then had I built the courage. In our house, questions were rare, I'd never heard anyone else ask such a thing. By nine, however, curiosity overtook unease. My father was out too, which helped, my mother was more malleable when he wasn't around. The whole house, in fact, changed in his absence, as though all the curtains opened an inch or two wider.

'What do you mean?' my mother replied. She was cleaning the kitchen with a number of liquids that she lined

up on the counter in order of use. Some were branded products decanted into nondescript bottles; others were filled with her own concoctions, plants and herbs grown in the garden, brought together in her own secret
chemistry.

For daytime cleaning, she used seven liquids; after dinner, only three.

'Father Henry told me,' I said. 'But I don't know what it means.'

She continued her spraying and scrubbing, moving exactly as she would had I not been there at all.

'It means…that he knows what is right. Even when it is difficult, or sacrifice is required – even when others think he is wrong.'

She returned to her line of bottles beside the sink.

'But how does he know?' I said, barely resisting the urge to tug on her apron, distract her more effectively from her task. 'How does he know what is right?'

'Because he is a good man,' she said immediately. 'A good man knows.'

'What if he knows what is right but acts differently? Would he still be a good man?'

Only then did she pause and just for a second. 'Are you saying your father does act differently?'

I too stopped, realising that if I did believe in his goodness, I wouldn't have asked the question at all, that we wouldn't be stood in this kitchen, breathing sterile air.

'No,' I said. It was all I could say, before racing upstairs.

I barely found a sock in time.

*

Poppy slept a lot the week after our father died. She napped in the garden; I had to wake her when the shade passed.

Her skin was so thin, I could trace the blood vessels travelling beneath, it couldn't be left to burn. Even with my help, her cheeks freckled, her collarbone grew pink. She was tranquil when she slept, but woke jaggedly as though from a bad dream. When I asked, however,
She denied dreaming at all.

My mother said it's normal, that the baby was taking and taking, that even if Poppy made more, the baby would take that too.

'Can't she make it stop?' I asked, aware that I was too old for such a question. My mother laughed, acknowledging my silliness in a way she wouldn't have
before he died.

'You don't want it to stop,' she said. 'You want to give it everything.'

*

I had once hoped for a very different life. I would go to the city to study, and never leave, for I'd heard it was a place where lights stayed on all night, and people talked and laughed and opened themselves instead of closing tight. I would smoke cigarettes and kiss boys, and kiss girls. Streets and flats and buildings, all burgeoning spaces where my father
was not.

Sometimes, this life was so veritable, I could smell the fumes, hear the sirens, dance to the music; I could live my life behind my eyes, all the while aware of its
nothingness.

But I could never leave Poppy, would never. Not in the place that
he was.

*

I was twelve the next time I asked my mother.

We'd just returned from church where Father Henry had spoken of goodness as godliness; he said one could act in a godly way, but his heart must also be pure.

'Does that mean Dad is godly?'

I pictured the charred pages of the bible, massacre and ruin, above all

punishment.

My mother took off her scarf and hung it atop her coat. She rubbed her neck where it had been, as though it had been made not of tender chiffon but strong hands, pressure in the very tips of the fingers.

'Don't ask me this again.'

*

'Do you think it's a boy?' I asked Poppy. 'Or a girl?'

It was clearly the first time she'd considered this.

'I don't mind,' she said, finally. 'It is mine.'

I sat down beside her on the hot, crisp grass. 'Does that mean we are his?'

She turned toward me in a rare moment of eye contact, of

understanding.

'Not anymore.'

*

By sixteen, I had learned my tolerance for pain, I had learned

what I was willing to endure

for what gain.

But questions were difficult, I couldn't ensure the answers would be worth their consequences.

Still, I asked my mother, two years before he died – though this time my words changed in my mouth.

'Is my father a good man?' I said, my tongue suddenly bigger and thicker, as though it sought to
suffocate.

My mother leant her forearms on the kitchen top she scrubbed each day with seven different liquids and stared into the garden she tended with both love and emphatic precision.

'Your father has ruined my life,' she said, her gaze glued to her plants, the damp buds of liquid on their leaves.

I felt the bile begin to rise again but for the first time I was able to swallow it down, I flattened my insides, stiff and unyielding as they were – I made them
yield.

*

When Poppy told me she was pregnant, I felt a sudden urge to
hide,
as we had when we were young, hours spent seeking small spaces where we could reduce ourselves, folded, invisible. I never felt fuller than when tangled up with my sister beneath furniture, inside cupboards, in the hollows of trees, at once protecting and
protected.

She used simple words, and few of them, as if that would lessen their impact; but I heard as if she'd screamed. There was no one purer of heart.

I stared at her belly, imagining the reaction inside that had made something new, something separate yet not,
minute cells, defenceless
yet with such power.

My mother had never come with us, never hid, or ran to trees, or watched the contents of my stomach splash across the alley wall. But that day, I heard a tremor behind the door and, looking back, I realise she had finally joined us.

*

Poppy and I walked that afternoon, as we often did. When we got home, the house seemed oddly still. I don't know what I'd expected, perhaps wildfire or flood. But all was quiet, even when I went inside, wandered the rooms, lighter than they'd ever been, full of August sun and the smell of cut grass. I could have heard a spider's steps, so
complete
was the silence.
Eventually, I found my mother in the kitchen, putting away her sprays in the exact order she retrieved them. I didn't think she'd noticed me until she murmured;
'It's lucky he took no notice of my garden.'

*

We buried my father on a Tuesday.
A window, perhaps, opened next door, a face in the placid night that would discard this scene just as they had my socks. We lowered the body into its rightful place, and with it, all its ceaseless severity.
'You did a good thing,' I told my mother.
'Mercy shall follow me all the days of my life,' she said, scattering a few seeds that tapped along his rigid spine.
They matter, I think.
The details.

The Last Walk

Lesley Bungay

She had little time. They would be here at 2 o'clock to take her away. Away from the house with the stairs she could no longer manage and the large garden that was too much for her. It was a year ago that the dining table and six chairs were removed, and a single bed brought downstairs for her to sleep amongst the china cabinet, the bookcases and the self-assembly clothes rail. Jean from Homecare came once a week on Friday to help her upstairs for a bath; other days she made do in the downstairs cloakroom. They were right of course, her son and his young second wife, the ground floor room at Spring Falls, with its modern ensuite bathroom complete with sit-in shower, would be perfect for her.

In the five years since her Joe died, Ollie came once a week on Saturday to mow the grass and keep the garden pruned and weed free. Like his grandpa, he had borne her instruction with patience, and she'd enjoyed those afternoons together, mingled with frequent breaks for tea and biscuits. In the summer months they'd wait in anticipation for the familiar melody of the ice-cream van 'boys and girls come out to play' and she'd feign surprise at finding a few coins in her pocket. At almost eighteen and eighty the delight at the pretence did not diminish. Now he'd gone to university and the icy winter had kept her indoors, nursing arthritic joints. They were right of course, the ground floor room at Spring Falls with its small terrace of pots and planters full of neglected shrubs and overgrown perennials, would give her plenty to do in the coming summer months.

She washed up the single plate and the single cup and sat in the wingback chair by the patio doors to wait. Her small suitcase stood ready by the front door. No need for her to pack much, only a few essentials needed. Robert would sort out the house and Alice would make sure she had what she needed, clothes and a few photographs and perhaps an ornament or two.

She looked out over her garden. It had been like marshland when they moved in fifty years ago, a wet winter on newly dug ground. Joe described it as a mud bath, for her it was a distraction, a new project after the injury that prematurely ended her career. She digested books by famous horticulturalists, took inspiration from magazines and was amongst the first to watch Percy Thrower create his gardening world. With the solitary Ash tree that stood at the far end of the garden for company, she planned, plotted, and planted. Joe obliged at weekends by erecting a shed and a greenhouse. He dug borders where she asked and laid a meandering path from the patio, the full fifty-metre length, to the Ash tree. When her boys arrived, the far end of the garden was filled with a wooden climbing frame and slide. Protected from the summer sun under the dappled shade of the bower, it became a pirate ship, a fort and a den.

She had a little time; she could manage one last walk. She pushed open the double doors. The spring sun was warm and inviting. The sound of the breeze rustled in the newly unfurled leaves of the Birch trees that ran along the boundary. The ubiquitous robin chirped along to the click, click, click of her walking sticks on the stone path, keeping time with her decreasing pace. She stopped at the first border, unable to resist the impulse to deadhead daffodils. She'd planted hundreds over the years. Every autumn on her hands and knees, bulb after bulb added to the spring illumination of the flowerbeds when all else was dead and brown. Her favourite was a Narcissus papyraceus, its delicate clusters of paper white petals stood out against the golden yellow and orange of the traditional jonquils. They'd come from the Isles of Scilly, the final holiday with all four of them together. Bobbie, as he preferred then, was seventeen and studying for A-levels, James at fifteen, was determined to leave school to join the army. Her boys were becoming men, but in that summer of messing about in boats and snorkelling with seals she saw a glimmer of the children they had once been.

With two sticks held precariously in one bent hand she stooped to pinch the faded flowers, crooked fingers stuffing the shrivelled trumpets into her cardigan pocket. The exertion was too much for her crumbling spine and as she clutched her back to ease the effort of straightening, one stick loosened from her weakened grasp and fell to the ground. She held tightly to the other with both hands waiting for the spasm to subside before walking on.

Stacks of unsown seed trays lay undisturbed in the greenhouse covered in woven silver threads. Smells of decaying tomato vines lingered in the warm stale air as she slid open the door. An habitual act of ventilation, but unnecessary; she knew nothing would be nurtured within the glass this year. She reached for the wooden bench that stood by the vegetable patch, welcoming the brief rest. She recalled the joy on Bobbie's face when he dug up his first harvest of potatoes, and James' cheeky grin when she caught him eating peas raw from the pod. When the digging became too much for Joe, Robert had built some raised beds from reclaimed sleepers, so that they could manage to cultivate some lighter crops, dwarf beans and salad. He had toiled on them for weeks between work and visits to the hospital and finally the hospice. Manual work helped keep his mind off the inevitable, he said.

She ran her finger around the red rings on the rotting arm of the bench from the many glasses of wine consumed there. The seat was strategically placed to catch the late evening sun and they'd often reward themselves with a glass or two after an industrious day. The lawn already needed cutting, except in the bare patch. The one place she'd allowed Ollie to kick a ball around with his grandpa without the risk to bloom or pane. She pictured his chubby legs in candy-striped shorts beckoning her to join them. 'Come Grammy,' he said but by then her displaced hips would not endure kicking the lightest of balls.

The sound of a lawn mower starting up in a neighbouring garden broke the quiet and she soon smelled the fresh green scent, the first of the year. It enticed her and she slipped off her shoes, using the end of her one stick to remove the socks from her bunioned feet. The blades of grass slipped between each misshapen toe that wriggled with delight at their freedom. She pushed herself to standing once more, wincing as her knees protested. With the mossy ground cushioning each step, she carried on.

She paused at the Magnolia soulangeana as she always did. Each goblet shaped blossom had succumbed to the late frost; the pink blush faded on withered ivory petals that hung lifeless, their beauty gone too soon. She'd planted it for James, one year to the day that he departed for The Gulf. She preferred to remember that day, seeing him standing in his uniform, his face glowing with pride to serve his country. That day and not what followed. On each of the twenty-nine anniversaries since, she wept for the man he should have become and the body never recovered, left to the desert dust.

There was still dew in the grass and the dampness penetrated her feet, numbing the extremities. She shuffled on to the rose bed, yet to bloom, each tight bud a promise of delicate pastels and flamboyant reds that she would not see this year. Each chosen for their name: A Shropshire Lad, vigorous and strong, towering over the centre obelisk; by its side was Ballerina, a small shrub with blossom pink flowers and a light fragrance; the bridal white of Winchester Cathedral, the rambling Bobbie James; Geoff Hamilton, her favourite; Audrey Hepburn, his; Ruby Wedding and Absent Friends, each a reflection of their life together. The Jane Austen Rose, the final one, the one that held bittersweet memories. Bought at Chawton House, their last outing together. A birthday lunch at Cassandra's Teashop in the village, followed by a stroll around the house and gardens. The summer sun had warmed her bones and she'd felt comfortable and at ease at the iconic author's home. But digging the hole for the purchased rose was Joe's final effort. She had lain on the ground beside him, feeling his body fade into the earth, wanting the grass to curl around her fingers and toes and draw her in too.

She reached the row of evergreen Skimmia japonica that lined the back of the garden, one to mark the graves of each of the pets that had come and gone from their lives. The dense panicle clusters were beginning to open and she breathed in their heady scent. There had been two rabbits when the boys were young, succeeded by two Labradors and finally her Westie. Her last reason for remaining in her own home; dogs weren't allowed at Spring Falls.

She was there. The towering tree held pride of place at the back of the garden. Always later to come into leaf, its skeletal branches swayed above her, the ends swooping up towards the clear, calm sky. She patted the rough trunk like an old friend. Tracing her fingers over the contours and furrows, she approved of how they blended with the raised veins and creases of her own hand. The bark yielded to her touch, feeling soft and penetrable. She watched as her hand sank into the wood. She withdrew with a gasp. Then, letting the second stick fall to the ground, she grasped the ancient tree with both hands, watching as her skin blended with the ageing timber.

She had no time. She could hear the car pulling up on the gravel driveway. She leant into the tree watching her forearms disappear from sight.

She heard Robert call, 'Mum.'

She stepped in closer, touching the trunk with her bare feet, watching as the timber surrounded her toes as if she was standing on wet sand.

Then the irritation in Alice's voice, 'Where is she? We need to be leaving now.'

She turned and pressed her back against the trunk feeling it embrace her. Her limbs weightless, her joints pain free, her body at one with the Ash. She took one final look and closed her eyes.

They were right, of course, her son and his young second wife. She could leave her house, but she would never leave her garden.

The Summer Splits in Two

Shelley Roche-Jacques

She remembers the splash. Remembers half this, half that, fighting for attention in her flustered brain – then coming to her senses, clambering out of the empty bathtub and running to the balcony, pulling up her knickers and shorts. Remembers dazzles and flashes of her brother's body flailing in the swimming pool below. Then struggling to propel herself down the twisting tiled staircase, held back by a sickening force, like in a dream.

She remembers the day before, the force of heat as they'd stepped off the plane – like opening the oven door, when Mum wasn't looking, to see if the cake had risen. Then the coolness of the holiday apartment – the whirring ceiling fans – a world away from last year's rainy caravan in Wales.

The afternoon of the second day, being told to watch Danny *just for an hour, okay?* while Mum and Roy went to the taverna round the corner, where men sat watching girls go by.

She remembers Danny busy-busy at the pool table on the terrace, lining up the balls, click-clicking them methodically round the edge of the table – his new holiday routine. Remembers how he had to edge his body along one side of it because there wasn't really room for a pool table next to the swimming pool. *Pool – Pool*, Danny had said, pointing from one to the other.

She'd been agog, she remembers, when Roy had smugly announced that the apartment he'd booked would have its own swimming pool. The freedom of charging up and down the length of it – a world away from the swimming baths at home where boys dive-bombed and dunked each other and made dirty jokes about swallowing and spitting and splitting girls in two.

She remembers wandering upstairs to Mum and Roy's bedroom to absentmindedly snoop – their balcony overlooking the terrace – looking down at Danny, almost a fully-grown man now, still at the pool table carefully shunting the balls, click-clicking and pool-pooling to himself. She remembers the ensuite with the big round bath – and standing in the bath to reach a slatted cupboard to get a closer look at something hot pink she'd spied through the slats. Remembers the thrum in her chest, and how strangely solid, heavy, jelly-like the object in the cupboard was. And other intriguing items – big silver beads and something like a bottle-stopper with a pink crystal top. Remembers sitting down with them in the empty bath – the thrumming – the feeling of being on the brink – a world away.

She remembers the splash. The jolt back. The dizzying aerial view from the balcony. The treacherous tiled staircase like a horrible dream.

She remembers the cold shock of the pool, the grabbing and wrestling and going under, and resurfacing, and gasping – the pulling and heaving and heaving, the strength coming from god-knows-where, and finally getting Danny's body, bigger than hers, up, out of the heaviness of the water, him purple and coughing and wanting Mum. Wrapping him in a towel, collapsing with him in a heap on the terrace. Saying *Okay, you're okay, you're okay*. She remembers remembering the things left out in the big round empty bath upstairs

76

– stranded – sickeningly stranded – as Mum and Roy came back.

She remembers, that night, she should have felt happy; grateful and giddy with relief. But instead guilt lay on top of her; its full watery weight. The future still before her like a twisted, slippery staircase.

Impressionism

Emma Timpany

Last night I dreamt I stole blueberries from your freezer, lifted them from the mist and frost as if from a sarcophagus of ice. I must explain that I have never stolen anything in my life, but, in my dream, I had conned my way into your house by offering to do your cleaning. Whilst inside, I filched the blueberries and wrapped them in my teal blue dressing gown, which lay, with dream logic, nearby. Though the blueberries were frozen, somehow I'd left evidence, a trail of dull, purple handprints, and I used the cord of my gown to wipe all traces away.

In the kitchen, while your back was turned, I took some loose change from the jar of coins on your counter before smiling, saying goodbye to you, and hurrying home. As for you, you looked at me with utter suspicion, no witness to my crimes and yet aware that I was guilty.

I think of you infrequently, perhaps once or twice a year, but lately I've been preoccupied by might-have-beens. We had the necessary qualifications for friendship—similar interests, mutual friends—yet friends we never were. It's rather like getting an ear worm, not being able to stop singing an irritating tune: however much you hate it, it's stuck in your brain, driving you mad. And it's not as if anything actually happened, so why is it bothering me?

All this began a few weeks ago, when your name started

cycling through my head one Friday night. I was up late and alone on the sofa (in the same teal blue dressing gown, thinking I should get up and go to bed, because I don't usually sit on the sofa alone late at night, but I couldn't seem to start moving). After your name appeared, I thought of the fairy cakes, dry in my throat, and the children, who are so much bigger now, as they were then, pressing shapes into play dough, on that day so long ago when my voice got stuck.

How had it happened? The dryness, the stuck words, after the fluency of our first meeting, that silky, exciting conversation that flowed like water over smooth, smooth pebbles, that ranged from Antarctica to Iceland, from Dunedin street names to that thin place, Iona, from mermaids to bathtubs, all of it lost, dissolved, crumbs in my throat I couldn't swallow then, crumbs I still can't swallow.

In our old house, near the end of the corridor which led from the front door to the kitchen, was a dining room. The room was dark and yet I always liked it. Its low sash window looked out into a courtyard filled with pots of plants which tolerate low light—a *Fatsia japonica*, ferns, a *Viburnum tinus*.

We sat in this room the day you came to visit. I had made fairy cakes, and the children helped me to ice them. I got the nicer cups out, the ones without chips on their rims. I was thinking, I suppose, of the way we used to do things in Dunedin when we'd go round to visit friends. There was always tea made in a pot and vintage plates and cups before they were fashionable. We used them because we were poor, living in flats, and most things we owned and used—crockery, cutlery, clothes, furniture—was second hand; strange that everyone wants it now, this old stuff,

80

the patterned plates and cups. There were always cakes, made or bought, to show you'd made an effort, to show your visitor you cared. And, in fact, the darkness of the room was also like the darkness inside some of those old Dunedin houses, so perhaps I was trying to recreate something without realising it, to scroll backwards fifteen years to an earlier time in my life.

So, as you could have seen, had you noticed, I had been looking forward to seeing you, had made an effort with the cups and cakes, and I'd tidied, but you didn't seem to notice anything; you seemed uncomfortable, said little. You knew I had children but still, they seemed to surprise you. Or perhaps it was the house, a little, shabby, ordinary terrace house, the walls of the dining room covered in glittery children's handprints, drawings, paintings.

That table was where so much happened: every meal and every making session, paying bills and working out budgets. Earlier in the day, I'd filled old ice cream tubs with sand and spread play dough on trays and the children had made shapes in them, pressing down anything they could find, and then filling the spaces with feathers, with torn up pieces of paper. As I sat there with you, I was tired for the usual reasons; another broken night, another early start, a busy morning, breakfast, snacks and lunch, frantic tidying up and making the blasted cakes.

You'd wanted to come at three in the afternoon, a bit of a dead time, the older child flagging but no longer taking a nap, the younger one unable to settle because of the unusual activity—three in the afternoon was the time of fair-weather walks, of rocking-to-sleeps, of desperate afternoon videos. A cup of tea and a cake and a little, listless chat—no mermaids this time, no gold pouring onto a Hebridean beach from a nearly accessible heaven—and me feeling for the first time all that I wasn't, hollow, transparent as a pillar of light, but not in a good way (not with the pure emptiness of a saint or the rewarded deprivation of an ascetic) but because I was seeing myself as you saw me. Then, after crumbling some cake in your fingers, after half an hour perhaps, you went and after that I did not hear from you for such a long time.

So long ago but, when I think of it, I can feel my younger child's small body pressed against mine, see my older child's dazzling smile and sparkling eyes and hear her bright talk—the smell of them, the weight and touch of them, which all these years on I still feel in my left hip as an ache.

The first time we met was at a reading group. It took place in a café, an upstairs room, one of the oldest buildings in town, Jacobean, maybe, which would have been here when Byron walked these streets. We talked about Iceland and holy wells, old tin baths set before the fire, the darkness inside those Dunedin villas, an orange-enamelled teapot filled with red-pink camellias we both remembered on the kitchen table of one of those houses, and I said to myself, *I've made a new friend.*

But now I think about it, I'd seen you even before that, reading an excerpt from your novel and seven (or is it eight?) years later it's just been published. And I wouldn't have known, but I was sitting on the sofa late at night and your name started running through my head, repeating and repeating, though I hardly ever think of you, and so I went to the computer and looked you up and there it was, the news that your book had been released that very day.

And I started to think again about what had happened between us, which was nothing of course, and why I had ended up feeling hurt by it and slighted. I still feel uneasy thinking of us sitting around that table, the cake sticking in my throat, the words drying in my mouth. And of sitting in another dark room where my computer was, sending emails that you didn't often respond to, or, if you did, only after days, weeks even, had passed.

At times I wonder what my life might have been like with different echoes coming back rather than the sound of my footsteps passing outwards, unimpeded, towards some far edge, and I remember how you spoke of what you called the perfect quiet; it occurred sometimes during a performance, a quality of listening that could tell you whether you were on the right track. That's what I'm doing here, writing into the silence, waiting to hear what doesn't come back.

Another friend came into my life, some-one with whom I did not have much in common except we both had children, and after that I was ill with an infection which took months to shift. I remember it as one of my lowest times. Then came another disaster which submerged my life for four whole years. I stopped caring about anything unnecessary.

The last time I saw you, a friend invited me to one of your events. You'd moved on by then, were living overseas. You read some new work and I listened to you, and I listened to the audience listening to you; I listened to see if I could hear that quality you'd described. I couldn't, and I wondered whether what you were trying to write would one day become good, or whether, like so many other things that had barely had a chance to happen, your heart had already gone out of it.

Hold Still

Margot McCuaig

Your story about winching the *stunner fae Belfast* is stop-start; interrupted when you take tiny sips from a can of fizzy Irn Bru. The sweetness is wafting in my direction and nausea stings, but the moment passes and I blink, focusing on the road I am driving. I shiver and ask *how can ye drink that stuff* but you shrug as if I need therapy for my indifference.

It is eight in the morning and the sun is high, but I cannot see it because sea fog is engulfing the shoreline and lingering on the road along the coast. The day is running away. The ferry is sashaying through Loch Ryan and I drive as though I were on board, my car riding alongside it until the road ascends and I lose the Antrim Princess to trees keeping secrets in the hills above the loch. The fog horn is absent despite the mist but I hear it anyway, a warning settling in my ears. I shake my head and silence fills the space, as though I've just dropped the sea shell I was clutching against my cheek.

I am tired. Quiet. *Too quiet*, you say just as the car engine growls and you think you have to repeat what you said. This time, I can feel your intense stare. You are urging me to look at you but I do not give in. My car coughs like an old man and you laugh, distracted, or maybe you're relieved to escape the intensity, because I am being intense. I can feel it in the way I'm fighting urges too, willing – not willing – willing – not willing my fingers to peel their grip from the steering wheel and let the car speed over the cliff. For a split second I imagine sea demons snapping at my heels as we sink into the water and then I return to business, bracing my shoulders and pushing my foot to the floor, making the car climb the hill with my own sheer strength.

I glance in the rear mirror and Ailsa Craig is like a watching ghoul in the sea behind us. I search for a different distraction, turning the attention back to you and the body you coveted a few hours before.

Never mind batting back tae me. I need mare detail oan the wee Belfast fella. I muster enthusiasm in my voice, trying to feign a Belfast accent for fun, but it isn't enough. You can hear the thinness of my voice. I mistakenly take my eyes from the road and glance at you. You are watching me. I want to ask you if you know you're staring at an effigy, but you don't give me the chance. It's your turn to talk.

Yer always so down these days you say *sadder, even, than when …* You don't finish and you turn to the window, but that is fine. More than fine. The minutes pass by and you move on in your mind. I can tell you are watching for deer in the valley so you can shout, *look, there's hunners of them* knowing I can't look because I am trying to keep my eyes on the road. I'm not succeeding well in that task either. Rosebay willowherb and meadowsweet are teasing in lay-bys. I wipe saliva from my mouth and swallow longer than I need to, craving the taste of something other than the hard shell of reality.

I drive on, the gears crunching loudly as my left foot misses the bite more often than I care for. I'm a new driver, but I'm a driver. Thanks to my dad who painstakingly ensured I learned as soon as I turned seventeen, encouraging me softly as I ran his Citroen into the ground and almost into the river at the end of our road. The day I nearly crashed, Dad brushed off my embarrassment with the offer of ice-cream. *We need fresh air, hen,* he said, locking the car door and placing the key in his pocket. We followed the line of the river along Dundrennan Road, then turned right into Carmichael Place. We walked for a short distance and then Dad's tone changed. He tangled his fingers in the long strands of his beard and turned away from me, watching something I couldn't see.

Whit's up? I remember asking Dad when he finally looked at me. *This is where Patricia Docker wis found, hen. Murdered by another bastart that got away wae it. I'm no gonnae utter the filthy name the press gied him,* he said. He had to though, as I didn't know who he meant. I cried when he told me and I curled my fingers around the sodden neck of my t-shirt in search of comfort. *Listen tae me,* he said, turning his tongue over and over in his mouth. *Never use that fuckin piece of shit phrase in the same breath as the names o' the lassies. Ah don't need tae tell ye they don't deserve it.*

Dad spoke with such softness I had to lean in close to be sure I was hearing words and not the breeze picking up under the elms at the end of the lane. He asked me to promise and it wasn't a hard thing to do. We carried on in silence and when we stopped at the café, Dad pointed to a tenement flat above it. *Up there, hen, that's whir Patricia an' her wean lived. Wae her ma an' da. Her da learned aboot her murder in the papers. Cin ye imagine, finding oot like that? Air lassie almost hame, almost safe, but no making it.* I can imagine, but that wasn't Dad's point.

I had a question I didn't want to know the answer to, but I asked it regardless.

Did Mum know we lived so close tae where this happened?

She did, hen, an' she was terrified. Aw the fuckin time.

It was Dad's turn to cry, but I didn't have any consolation to offer him. We both know what happened to Mum, and clinging to each other outside that café wouldn't change her fate. It had done its dirty business two years earlier.

Even now Mum's fear is a feeling I can't shake. I'm consumed by it. I wonder if Mum knew that her fear was the one certain thing about her. Was she waiting for her imminent death, every minute of every day? But isn't that true for every woman? That we're just waiting for a man to kill us?

You bring me back, and even though I am grateful, I tremble as you push a tape into the rickety cassette player, slamming it hard with the heel of your boot to make it play. I don't instantly recognise the song, but in a few beats I know I'm hearing Pale Shelter by Tears for Fears. The car is filled with *you don't give me love.*

I drive to your parents' holiday house and park by the beach where we first met as girls. The sand is different in the fog. It looks frozen in time. I feel my eyes lift to sea and I exhale deeply, excited by how fiercely the cold would burn if the sea monster pulled me out beyond the tides.

We clamber from the car and you playfully stab your fingers into my ribs, like you've always done. Sharper than you need to, but you want my attention. I smile and feign surprise as though you have stumbled upon me, quite by chance. Then I settle my lips and stay silent. The first time I saw you is on my mind.

You were paddling barefoot, alone. Even though we were just kids on holiday, we sealed our lifelong friendship in that moment. And now you are abandoning the outside world to focus on me again. I dread to think what you can see.

Are ye okay, Enoch? you ask, your hand pushing into your pocket, searching for relief. There is every need for the doubt settling on your face, but you don't know that yet. I want to wait a little while longer before my pain pains you too. I kiss your cheeks, one then the other, reassuring you that nothing is different from this morning, or the mornings before it.

Dae ye want te walk up the road for a bit? you ask. I nod, following your lead, accepting your hand greedily when you pass it. You secure your fingers around mine and I squeeze tightly. There's hope in your touch and it is more than I can stand right now. My gait is reluctant and you think I do not want to be with you.

Dae ye want tae head back? Tae Kevin's? you say, and I nod, even though all I want is for this moment to be about you and me and not your boyfriend. So I pick up my pace and take the lead.

What wis his name? I ask *the Irish fella ye winched the face off in Stranraer.* You are laughing. You remember, but you are choosing not to tell me.

Why bother wae insignificant detail, you say, *he's in the past.*

I lengthen my stride and you hurry to keep in line. You're giggling hard, saying *you're walking faster than the wrecked car yer da gied ye.* You're calling after me, asking now that I've driven back, *are ye sober,* even though I drank myself to sleep after you disappeared with the boy whose name will not be remembered. We are about to cross the bridge over the river when you say *stop.* I think you're going to ask me to look at Granny's old house so I keep my eyes forward. But you don't. Perhaps you have forgotten she even existed. I can understand if you have. My maternal line is obliterated. It is only me now.

Let's climb the hill, hiv a wee hair o' the dug at the cave like the old days. You see the look on my face and laugh, thinking my head is somewhere else. *Don't be a daftie,* you say, *ghosts arenae real, they're just stories.* I nod because I agree. Once we are gone we are gone and there is nothing frightening in that. You keep talking and I listen. You say, *we can gie our legs a workout* and then you pause, drawing breath before you carry on.

An' then we can talk about whit's bugging ye.

Your face is pleading with me to give you what you want, even though you know I always do. I wonder if you want time with me or if you're avoiding Kevin, needing longer to wash the boy whose name you can't remember from your skin. Either is fine.

But whichever it is, you are asking too much. It wouldn't matter on any other day. You are asking me to go with you to the hill where I had the last meaningful conversation with Mum. Our last day of holiday. I was fifteen. She told me about a surprise she and Dad had planned for my birthday. I listened to her excitement, my face expressionless, too hormonal to tell her she couldn't have made me any happier. *Sweet Sixteen,* she said, *you an' me, an' ah mean just you an' me, yer dad's getting ditched fir this wan. We're going tae Spain oan a lassies trip, hen.*

A day later I yelled *bye then,* keeping my head under the duvet when Mum woke me earlier than I wanted to be woken to say she was going to work. She never came home and I stayed under that duvet until you crawled in beside me and held me tight.

It is the strangest coincidence that you want to go up the hill, today. Today of all days, when I have decided I want to be with Mum. Wherever it is she went when the end came.

I shudder and you turn to me. You look worried as you say *jeez Enoch, yer fuckin freezing.* I shake and you can

90

see you are right. I am cold, but I am cold because my heart is stone.

When you pull me close I fall into you and cry. You take your jacket off and rest it over my shoulders, then gently tease me into it, your touch as tender as the day you helped me block out the light under the duvet.

Enoch, ma beautiful pal you say *talk tae me, yer scaring me.*

I'm scared an' all, I tell you, and then I say, *an' I don't think I'll ever stop being scared.*

You ask me *did somewan hurt ye?* It's quite the thought, thinking that you can't see what's tearing me apart. *Helen,* I say, *I don't want tae be here anymore.* You speak, saying *we'll go back* and I stop you.

I'm no talking about here, walking up this fuckin hill, I don't mean that.

Your jaw drops and I fall with it, sinking to my knees. Perhaps you know what's coming before I say it.

I don't want tae be fuckin anywhere. You tighten your hold and I lean forward, stumbling when you release your grip and turn me round so I'm facing the field.

Look, Enoch, there's a horse o'er there, you say. I turn away, not understanding why that should matter. But you stroke my cheek, encouraging me to raise my eyes. I give in because I owe you one last act. *It's a sign* you say, and I shake my head wildly, strangely aware that the bloody horse is doing the same. *Mind that poem?* You are speaking quickly, too excited for this moment, and I can't understand this triumphalism in you. You've got your hands under my oxters now, raising me to my feet. I let you lift me, knowing it isn't hard because I am weightless for the first time since Mum was murdered.

Fir fuck sake, Enoch, I know ye remember it fae school.

You're running now, and I'm chasing you, like I'm in the

air. When we reach the horse you take my hand and place it on its muzzle. It's only when I lean in close that I hear it.

Since then they have pulled our ploughs and borne our loads

But that free servitude still can pierce our hearts.

Our life is changed; their coming our beginning.

Don't you say, pressing your finger against my lips. The sweetness of your perfume lingers as you take your hand from my face and jab my ribs. I don't smile, but I don't cry either. Stepping neither forwards nor backwards, I hold still.

Secrets

Mona Dash

You like the sound of the gravel beneath your feet. Crunch, crunch, like Toby's cereal, crispy cornflakes in frothy milk. The house is set right back, hidden behind trees.

'Is this the right address? You're not confusing them, are you?' Michael asks in his usual manner. He laughs and adds, 'That would be so you.'

You don't react. Instead you point at the sign on the porch and say, 'I am sure it's this one. Tile Cottage.' The sign is hanging askew, and he impatiently reaches out and straightens it.

'Toby, now come on!' Toby is hanging on your arm and you almost trip on him. The rain has been steady all morning and your heels sink into the squelch. Not practical attire for this weather, but since when have you been practical?

Someone steps out from a side door.

'Hello, Mrs Smith? I am Debbie, from the agency.' An elegant woman, dressed in a smart black skirt suit, a few wrinkles around her eyes.

'Hi, Debbie! Lovely house,' you say, even though you haven't seen anything of it.

'It's the first viewing I am doing here, and it's a quirky house indeed.'

'Quirky is good,' you smile enthusiastically, the way you are meant to on house viewings.

'The owners are on holiday, so it's just me. Young man, shall we go in?' she asks Toby.

Toby lowers his chin and doesn't look up. He doesn't want to look at new houses, even though you have explained a house with a larger garden would be nicer for him. Michael wants to invest in a bigger property and rent out the semi-detached you are living in now. And you, well, you want something different. You want rooms to rearrange, to become something more. You want alcoves and nooks. Instead of the smooth neutral walls, you want bumpy recesses. You want to hang threads of garlic and pans from a trellis in a large stone-floored kitchen. You want to bake cakes, stir soups, in a kitchen with warm burnt-orange walls. You want to dream, to morph into someone else.

Debbie opens a door off the living room. 'A little corridor down to a lovely living space! This house is full of secrets!'

And you can see that. The walls are curved; it's like going up a lighthouse. A narrow window is dug deep and on the wide windowsill, a picture of a little girl with blond curls stares out of its silver frame. It pulls at your throat. Toby is five now. People ask, just the one, too lazy were you, where's your second? They comment good-naturedly. They don't know. The miscarriages over the years – the clots of blood passing out like lumps of strawberry jam – your mind holding on in vain to what your body is bent on discarding. The still-borns, the beating, throbbing hearts suddenly quiet, the living warmth turning cold. For years, you had seen blood everywhere. You'd felt it flowing between your legs when there was none, you saw bloodied sheets when you tried to sleep. Your nightmares were soaking red. The insides of a fig, tendrils of pink bits, made you sick. Until Toby. And then the smiles! The joy of blowing raspberries, the clean baby smell, so much happiness at having him, that you didn't want anything anymore for a while. But now you do. You want a new life. You feel the emptiness in your stomach, never to bear, never to be full and round, walk with those sluggish, heavy pregnant-steps, yet you don't dare risk going through that again. Michael is done with seeing you weeping silently, sitting still on the sofa, moping a loss which was never to be. 'No more trying, no more babies, we must move on,' he had said, two years ago.

'This is the master bedroom.' A velvet red bedspread is draped on the large bed. Suddenly an image of John flashes before your eyes, you and John, on a bed.

'And just here, tucked in this corner,' Debbie opens two doors, 'the WC here, and the bath on the left.'

'Hmm, so it isn't all in one bathroom,' Michael says.

'You could break the wall down,' you hear yourself say. This sets them off. They discuss if it is a supporting wall or not.

'We can ask John,' you say.

John knows these things, gardens, houses, anything solid. You have known John for years. You have known John-and-Lydia even longer. – Lydia. Best friend from university. When she had moved back from up north and bought a house fifteen minutes away, with her husband John, the four of you met often. You had wept on Lydia's shoulder after yet another miscarriage, two years after Toby. Then Lydia had her cancer diagnosis. You watched her suffer, get well, falter, and ever so frail, melt away faster than ice-cream cones on summer days. She passed on in six months. Cervical cancer can be brutal.

John. You baked cakes, brought him wine, tucked him into the duvet, saw his tears. Over the years he recovered, became his solid self, always there to help, but still alone.

When the dimmer in the living room didn't work, when a wasp's nest appeared in the shed, when the kitchen drawer had to be fixed, he came over and sorted it all for you. And when you lost what wasn't meant to be, the third time, you'd held on to him, soaked his t-shirt wet with your tears, the huge bouquet of lilies he had brought, soft on your face. Sometimes Michael doesn't even know something needs to be repaired and it is done.

Last week, after you'd dropped Toby at school, you went over to John's. Your laptop screen had developed hairline cracks. John ordered a replacement screen, so there you were, at nine in the morning, in your crinkle cream dress. And John all fresh shower smells, in a crumpled blue tee and his faded ripped jeans.

As he worked in the study, you'd wandered over to the conservatory. A thick rubber plant in the corner, its leaves waxy and spilling over from the pot; orchids in many colours. Once he had presented you with some potted orchids, but they wilted, and then died. Plants, fish, everything, they just die in your house, as if the air isn't conducive to life.

You'd bent down to a shrub, the white wax petals tight in a cluster and breathed from the flowers. A sweet smell of jasmine. You wanted to fall into the smell, to drown in the flowers, or the rain, or the earth, or anything. You kept your head bowed, you wanted to stay there forever, you wanted to sink, like a stone.

'Leela! I fixed it, laptop's good as new. All sorted.' John's footsteps fast and hurried. Then a pause and his voice softer, 'Leela, are you alright?'

You are alright, you are never alright. You stood up close to him while his eyes, blue and anxious, scanned your face. You were the one who held his hands, the well-worn fingers that knew how to fix any loose tile, any bit of wood. He looked at you curiously and when you started kissing, you couldn't remember who had moved first, who had swept away the years past, who had brushed away the memories, the foundation of your relationship. Later, your bodies had found each other in his huge bed, his fingers on your face, and he traced its outline as if he was carving wood, carefully, deftly. And it was much later, only when it was time to pick up Toby, that you had left.

'I have died, I will lie here forever,' Toby declares. He has flopped on the red carpet.

'Come on Toby, behave,' Michael says.

This house is speaking to you. The small study, the irregular bedrooms, a balcony running across it, you can see yourself here, hiding in its depths, spending mornings looking for secrets, stepping over the uneven pedestal into the kitchen.

You step outside into the garden.

Purple clematis blooms over a trellis, just like the one in John's garden. You'd once said it was your favourite colour and John had come by the next day with a variety of purple blooms for your garden, iris, clematis, even wisteria. A small pond is dug into the soil. You go closer, the water is dark, deep...you see a flash of red suddenly. You step back.

'Mummy, Mummy!' Toby is calling out. He's followed you outside and is pointing at a set of cherubs, near the pond, 'I can see their.... willies...' He can't stop laughing.

'Let's go back in,' you say. You are flustered.

'Why do the owners want to move?' Michael is asking Debbie.

'They are getting on, their daughters, all four of them have flown the nest. A lot has happened here, ... a few stories in this house ... my manager was telling me... It's seen many a life...'

'The pond...,' you start.

'Yes, there is a little pond. It's not hard to maintain, or you can even have it filled.' Debbie answers before you have framed your question.

'Are you alright?' Michael asks you impatiently. He turns to Debbie and tells her firmly, 'We will have a chat and get back to you.' Before she can ask him anything more, he says, 'Let's go home now.'

'Yay!' shouts Toby.

In the car, Michael says, 'It's a good-sized plot but we will need to get a lot of work done. An extension, strip the walls, and change all those green carpets. Is the house worth the asking price? I will have to work out a comparison tonight and...'

'Green carpets? They were red.'

He stares at you suspiciously. 'You OK? Have you been seeing things again? You have been acting stranger than usual all week.' Michael sees everything in black and white. When you got married, and everyone said opposites attract, you had smiled in agreement, but over the years, his sense of ordering everything in neat drawers makes your head hurt.

'Yes, yes, am fine. Just got confused, the bedspread was red...,' you don't dare bring up the pond.

Michael doesn't question anymore. He thinks things left undiscussed are things sorted.

Tonight, you toss and turn, you wake a few times in the night. Michael is fast asleep and snoring. The rain is steady, caressing the windows, the rooftops. Your dreams are hazy, making you restless. Memories, thoughts, moments, John, Lydia, Michael, Toby, the house, everything dances in your mind like a kaleidoscope. You don't know when you fall asleep.

Monday dawns as if a different country; it's sunny and hot. After you drop Toby at school and are driving back, John calls again. You ignore it. Holding you close that day, he said how he loves the curve of your arms, the way your nails are irregular. He loves children. He loves Toby. He has so much to give, and so do you. How easy would it be! Move out, move in. But... he loves Lydia still. And you love Lydia – so how could you, you ask yourself? You picture Michael's anger – 'Wasn't Lydia like your sister? Bitch!' You imagine Toby's confusion – divided weekends for the rest of his life, split houses. Then you think of growing old, you and Michael alone. Toby somewhere else with his girlfriend. A vision of a silent house, there's nothing you can talk about, no one to talk to. Michael with his excel sheets, his stocks. You sitting near the pond, alone, secrets submerged.

On an impulse, you turn into the lane, and drive to the house. You want to see it once more. The owners are away after all and it's unlikely Debbie would have organised a viewing this early on a Monday morning.

You walk up the driveway. It's like another world, and the house itself seems sunk in the ground, as if wanting to hide. Like you.

You walk towards the porch, this is trespassing, you could be put in prison you think. You walk round to the pond. You notice a bush full with deep red roses, the blooms heavy, next to the pond, a little bench. You dare yourself to look at it again....and again, you see it. Sparkling reddish, the sun catches the water today. As you keep looking in, you see it, a mosaic of tiles in the pond, different shades of red. That's all it was. You sit down and look in, now you see some fish. You can smell jasmine somewhere, just like in John's conservatory. A small shrub of white flowers is at your feet. Waxy clusters of jasmine. You miss John, you miss the way you feel less broken with him.

Suddenly your phone rings loudly in the silence. You get it out of your bag. You know who it is. You walk out quickly, your heels crunching into the gravel, your hair flying as you start to run. Just for now, you know what you must do.

You answer the call and say, 'John...'

Go To Gate

Catherine Smith

From her corner seat, through the huge windows, Angela watches a small plane take off in the distance, climbing silently through still, grey skies.

A baby starts to wail and Bob tuts, shakes his head. Angela adjusts her glasses, cranes her neck to see the Departures Board. The flight number is up there, but not the gate number. She checks her watch; twenty past four, so boarding is due in twenty-five minutes. She wishes there were still proper, audible announcements, when a clear voice would tell you what to do and when to do it. If it was up to her, she'd already be heading towards Gate 20, because the flight for Glasgow always leaves from Gate 20. She knows the way and she knows it can take ten minutes to get there. Her mouth feels dry, but she decides not to finish her bottle of fizzy water, because then she will need the toilet, and the toilets are five minutes away, and there will be a queue. There's always a queue for the women's toilets.

She looks through the window again. Another plane, a much larger one, has just left the ground. She envies the passengers, safely strapped in, already on their way to wherever they need to get to.

Bob is staring at his phone, his plump thumb swiping at the screen. He drains his pint glass, softly belches and mumbles, 'Pardon me.' Angela digs her fingernails into her palms. Stay calm, she tells herself, he'll sleep on the flight. Focus on seeing Sarah and Calum. They'll be waiting at Arrivals. As soon as she can put her arms around them both, and drink in the scent of her grandson's hair, and nuzzle his skin, she'll be fine. She'll have a whole fortnight of them. And all of this will be worth it.

She realises her husband is leaning forward, huffing, preparing to stand up. He's saying something, but it's noisy, difficult to hear. She turns towards him, and he says loudly, 'Might as well have another. Want one, love?'

She feels her chest tighten. 'There won't be time – '

'Glass of red?'

'No – you can have a drink on the –'

But he's already standing, shouldering his way towards the bar, slowly, a few steps forward, stopping then moving again, through clusters of people moving between the bar and tables. She feels bile rising. These days, he does everything so slowly. He says it's because he's laid back and she's up-tight, but increasingly, he seems to take pleasure in leaving everything until the last minute, whilst she silently sweats and fumes.

He'd insisted they catch the train due to arrive at the airport barely an hour and a half before take-off. She'd wanted to take the earlier train, which would have given them at least two and half hours, in case there were any delays. 'Don't worry, love,' he'd said. 'Plenty of time.' He'd boarded it slowly, laboriously, puffing and sighing in that way he did so often these days. He'd heaved their suitcases onto the upper rack, so they were tricky to retrieve. She'd pressed her lips closed, looked out of the train window. If only he'd let her go on her own; if only he hadn't insisted she needed him to look after her. She was fine now she was on the Beta-Blockers. He resented the expense of flying to Glasgow but deemed the journey too far to drive. It wasn't as though he was particularly interested in his step-daughter or her child. Since Sarah left for Glasgow Art School, when she was nineteen, he'd professed himself baffled anyone could make a living out of 'those weird paintings.' He also thought having a baby using a sperm donor, 'without a father figure,' was irresponsible. He would spend most of the time sprawled on Sarah's sofa watching TV, or reading articles on his phone, while she, Sarah and Calum were out enjoying themselves.

If only he would leave her to her own devices, she'd happily arrive at the airport the *day* before, set up camp on one of those bench seats in the public area if necessary, because she would do anything – *anything* – to make sure she caught the flight. He'd been painfully slow checking in their case, too, trying to engage the poker-faced young woman on the desk in banter about weighing the passengers rather than the luggage.

He's making his way back from the bar now, both hands clutching his pint. Then he looms in front of her, places his glass on the table, grinning. He takes a packet of crisps from his pocket, drops that on the table, then thumps himself down on the seat beside her.

'Last chance of freedom before Sarah's rules,' he says, and she snaps back, 'She just doesn't like junk food around Calum, that's all.'

He chuckles. 'That's rich, considering they all live on deep fried Mars bars up there.'

She says nothing. He tears open the crisp packet, offers her one. She shakes her head.

Now, she wants to jump up, to walk off, to get away from him and his slowness, his silence, broken only by slurps of beer, as he scrolls through the news on his phone. She'd turned her own phone off, to save the battery, after her daughter's text wishing her a good flight, and telling her not to worry. She checks her watch. Nineteen minutes until scheduled take off. She squints up at the board. The gate number still isn't up there. Her chest feels tight.

He looks up, and pats her arm. 'Chill out, love,' he says. 'Are you sure you don't want a drink?'

Since he retired, three years ago, he's taken to saying 'Chill out' as a response to anything she finds difficult. Often, she wants to scream at him to show some urgency, to understand that his slowness, his passivity – these things are driving her mad. These things are *why* she needs medication. She veers between fantasising that she's won the lottery and can afford to leave him, and being ashamed of her own intolerance, because although he doesn't understand her and lacks any imagination, he's a good man, a kind man. When they met – ironically, he was the emergency plumber who quickly and calmly sorted out the washing machine which had flooded her kitchen – she'd been widowed for just over a year. Sarah was fourteen, stroppy, and the house fizzed with female tensions. She'd appreciated Bob's practicality, his patience. He never offered opinions on her parenting, and he didn't criticise Sarah. When he asked her to marry him, she felt safe.

But now, twenty years later, there are days when she wants to shove a red-hot poker up his arse.

He carries on his steady sipping, scrolling and chuckling. She checks her watch. The face is smeary, and she wipes it with the cuff of her jacket. Four thirty. Take off is supposed to be in fifteen minutes. She imagines Sarah telling her to breathe in slowly for five seconds, and out slowly for seven.

Suddenly, lots of people stand up, gathering jackets, bags, children, blocking her view of the departures board. A young woman nearby is saying, 'Gate 20, Christ that's miles, can you put Tilly in the buggy?' Angela jumps up and strains to see the board, and there's the flight number, BA 3587 to Glasgow, on time, that's it, it's been called. *Go to Gate 20,* the board is instructing. The backs of her hands prickle. She clutches her bag, shakes Bob's arm.

'Flight's been called,' she says. He makes a performance of putting his phone in his pocket. There's still a third of his pint left and he picks it up. She wants to slap him. She wants to dash the glass from his paw and smash it on the floor.

'Love,' he says, staring up at her, 'calm down. It's only the first call, they won't leave without us. Remember what the doctor said.'

She's fuming as he slowly drinks the remains of the beer while dozens of people begin their brisk journey to Gate 20. She wants to run after them, to say, I'm with *you,* not him. I'm punctual, I'm going to get to that gate in plenty of time.

She's aware of him puffing along behind her as she checks for the sign that says 'Gates 10-20', follows the briskly walking crowd, marches past the shops, towards the corridors with the huge windows overlooking the runways, where everyone is hurrying towards the gate.

Every sound is amplified: a suitcase's wheels squeaking, a baby crying, two young women, probably pissed, shrieking with laughter. She feels the blood banging in her temples. To her right, a series of departure lounges, full of people reading newspapers, studying their phones, running after their toddlers. Lucky, lucky bastards, all they have to do is wait to be called, there's no chance they will be too late. Gate 10, Gate 11. Why is Bob so slow, why did he have to have that extra pint?

They pass signs for male and female toilets and she can feel him slowing down and is sure that if he announces that he needs to stop for a pee, she will leave him there, she will not hang around outside the bloody Men's toilets. Keep going, keep going. Gate 12, Gate 13, Gate 14....

Outside, the skies are darker now, dirty dish-cloth coloured clouds gathering over the runway. Does that mean rain? Gate 15, Gate 16, another few minutes, come on, come *on*. She feels as though she's in one of those dreams where however fast you run, you never get to your destination, you find yourself on the wrong train or the wrong bus or your stop whizzes by and nobody hears you hammering at the window.

Gate 17, Gate 18, Gate 19.

And then, thank God, Gate 20, and she's in the long queue to show passports and tickets, to gain admission. Angela's heart is still thumping hard. As she nears the desk, she fumbles in her bag for her passport and ticket. Her hands are trembling as she hands them over. 'I thought I'd be late,' she says, and the woman in her neat navy and red uniform, her long brown hair swept into a bun under her pert little cap doesn't reply, but concentrates on scanning her passport and ticket, then says calmly, 'No, you're fine, Madam.' The electronic doors ping open. She's through.

She's sinking onto a seat when she realises she didn't check if Bob was behind her. For a few moments, she fantasises that he's not coming. He's changed his mind, heading back to the bar. He's letting her go.

But then he flumps down on the seat next to her, panting, his face gleaming with sweat. She can smell beer and crisps on his breath.

'Told you,' he says, patting her arm. 'Loads of time!'

On the plane, Angela's seat is by the window, and she tucks herself into it gratefully, stows her bag under the seat in front, pulls the seat belt into position, clicks it shut. Beside her, Bob grunts. His solid thigh is wedged against hers. She

106

lifts the arm-rest so that there is slightly more space between them. She feels weak, almost giggly, with relief, at being here. Seated, safe. The minutes she feared she'd lost – miraculously, not lost at all.

The engines start up, a steady rumble, and she feels the wheels beneath her start to turn. Bob's nearby hand is puffy and damp. She notices he closes his eyes through the sound of the captain's deep, soothing voice, welcoming his passengers, reassuring them they would take off just a little behind schedule, and asking them to pay close attention to the safety demonstration. She looks away from her husband, watches the slim young cabin crew man slip a bright yellow life jacket over his head, barely disturbing his neatly combed hair. He fastens the straps at the side, pulls out the red whistle, holds it to his lips. She realises that this part of flying has never worried her. She has never believed she'll be forced to don a lifejacket, be dropped into freezing water where she'll have to whistle for help, try not to pass out. What always scares her is being too late and the plane leaving without her. The humiliation and anger of watching it climb through the air, whilst she remains grounded. Howling.

Slowly, steadily, the plane lumbers along the runway. She closes her eyes and pictures Sarah, who she knows from recent texted photos will be thinner, with shorter hair than when they last met in the flesh, a year ago. She pictures her daughter smiling and waving, holding Calum's hand. Calum, with his long skinny legs and his shock of blonde hair and his slow, shy stare.

Now the engines are really roaring, the earth is tipping and through the window she sees the ugly terminal buildings and the huge car parks full of tiny cars and coaches fall away. The plane is climbing, climbing, high above the earth. What a miracle flight is, she thinks, how it accelerates time

– in about an hour and a half she will be in Glasgow, hundreds of miles away. Up, up, she counts the seconds – ten, fifteen, twenty, the plane is still climbing, everything at this odd angle, where all you can do is lean back and trust the pilot, trust the science of this thing called flight. Into the middle of grey clouds, where everything is fuzzy and indistinct, it's difficult to make out what's on the ground.

A minute or so passes. She's aware of Bob's warm, solid weight pressing against her shoulder. She turns from the window, irritated. Why does he always have to slouch?

Then she sees that his eyes are closed and his face is waxy. His lips are parted, as though he's about to chuckle. She looks at him more closely. He's completely still. She picks up his hand, resting on his belly and takes his wrist between her thumb and fingers. Seconds pass. There's no pulse. The plane is still climbing and the clouds are thickening. We took off, she tells herself, it's too late to turn back now. I made the flight. I'll get there.

Gently, she lets go of his wrist, places his hand back on his belly. The plane stops climbing and starts to level, the clouds disperse and suddenly, below her, there are green and ochre fields laid out like a carefully stitched patchwork quilt. And a river, the colour of beaten pewter.

Within these Walls

Ali Bacon

1068

My mother is standing in the centre of the room, her arms folded. Next to her is a man I have never seen before.

'The life of a nun is to be envied and admired,' she says. 'This gentleman will take you to England, to one of its greatest Abbeys.'

There are many questions on my lips but with this stranger amongst us (tall, bearded, eyes not unkind) I don't think they'll be answered.

The man says something to my mother in the Norman tongue and she speaks his words back to me. 'You will gain many skills, you will earn the love of God.' A pause. 'And the pride of your family.'

My family are curiously absent, my sisters sent to play in the muddy lane that leads off the square, my father in some conclave with the burghers of Ghent. The man has arrived unannounced. Between him and my mother there is something that speaks of familiarity. I sense his presence is not unexpected.

I am to leave with him the next day and I spend the later hours packing a small cloth bag, my mother standing over me.

'I don't understand.'

'You'll have more there than we can ever give you.'

'I want only what's here.'

Silence as she folds my winter cloak.

My father comes home and stares into his mug of ale. I've heard him say he has too many daughters but thought it was a jest.

'I am your eldest,' I say. 'Send Brigitte, send Beatrys.'

'They are too young.'

And he likes my sisters better. I have seen it in his eyes, a doting love he doesn't give to me. He prefers their blue eyes to my brown, their blond braids to the dark curls I inherit from my mother.

When I leave the house, riding behind my captor, father has left for his workshop. My mother stands by the door with my sisters around her legs. They are waving and calling to me, thinking I'll be back by nightfall.

On the deck of the ship, as the sea churns grey and foamy, I am heartsick but my breakfast stays down all the way to the other side and after another day's journey the stranger brings me to the Abbey at Wilton, leaves me with the Prioress, bids me goodbye.

I sleep in a dormitory. Woken in the darkness by the ringing of bells, I file with twenty others in our simple night shifts to the church. It is only later, at the office of Prime, that I see how the place is adorned with painted scenes. The Garden of Eden and Christ's passion on the cross: Heaven and Hell laid out before us, as if this can compensate for lives left behind.

The prioress makes me kneel in prayer.

Dear Father, Your ways are hidden from us. Make me compliant with Your will.

My lips speak the words but my heart cannot bend. In the reading hour I look out of the window. The fragrance of summer blooms is borne on the wind. I miss the stink of sheep dung and the noise of the city.

My name is Jeanne, but now I am to be Ursula. The Prioress says my compliance is all a matter of time.

The life of a nun is to be envied and admired.

First I must be found useful employment. The fire of defiance still burns in my head and my heart. Others see it as a cloak of flame and I am known as the unruly sister.

As the daylight hours grow longer, the other girls whisper to each other in the dormitory. I have learned only a few words of their language and no one chooses me as a friend. I stoke the flame of anger at my mother and her stranger for giving me to God.

Yesterday I was shown how to sow seeds in the garden, but as I worked I saw a chink in the wall and gazed through it to the fields unfolding around me, bordered with curled hedgerows. The prioress called me away. 'God's bounty is here within the walls. Don't strain at the leash.'

Today I work in the chapter house where the dexterous girls embroider soft silks. Those with broad fingers and a clumsy hand must stitch rough door hangings and hessian cushions. By Vespers I have blisters.

The sister in charge of sewing is called Maude and she tries to be kind. When I stab the edge of my thumb with the needle and suck at the spot of blood she puts her hand on my shoulder. 'One day you will find your place here,' she says. 'God finds no joy in your distress.'

The pain in my hands goes some way to quell my madness. But my fingers harden and the madness returns.

When I have been toiling in the chapter house for a month, Maude enters with a young woman. I have heard of her in the night-time whispering, the sister of a king who lost his throne. She is finely dressed and as fair as my sisters.

I attend to my stitching and I'm surprised when she pauses behind me. I look up. Her eyes are grey and almond-shaped and my face is reflected in them. Her name is Margaret, meaning Pearl.

We are told she will enter as a postulant and I'm startled by the leap of my heart and try to press it back where it belongs. A nun must not give in to unfettered feelings, but surely the desire for a friend is an innocent one.

In the reading hour I ask Margaret what has brought her to Wilton.

She answers without hesitation, 'The will of God.'

I am struck by the sudden knowledge that even my confinement could be part of His plan. I feel a different heat in my face, an acknowledgement of sin, while my eyes still prick with tears of defiance.

If Margaret knows of my shortcomings she says nothing and we sit together when we can. And in the following days I piece together the scraps of her story: her family's exile, her betrothal to a king, his marriage to another.

'You could have been a queen.'

'The cloister has more freedom than a castle or a court. I prefer the bosom of God to the currents that sweep my family from shore to shore.'

I tell her I was brought here against my will. Her eyes soften but her voice is steady. 'Prisons are of our own making, we must find freedom where we can.'

Questions about my mother and the stranger still fester in my heart, lying in wait to trouble me, especially in the hours of darkness. Only Margaret's presence calms me, her still and regal bearing, her gift of peace.

One day Maude finds me and takes me to the tannery where calf skins are flayed and flattened into parchment.

In an adjoining room the finished sheets are cut to size. My hand strays to a skin still hanging from the cross-bar, half way between the hide of a calf and the vellum of a written page. I feel the grain of its surfaces, the rough and the smooth, the animal in it tamed to new purpose.

Outside in the cloister, sisters sit at sloping desks, copying chapters and verses from the Bible.

'Hold out your hands,' Maude says and we look at my fingers, wounded in the jousts of altar-cloths and cushions.

'Each letter in the Gospel must conform to a perfect shape,' she says. 'Do you think you could learn to copy the Holy Books?'

I watch the scribes stretch their fingers and roll their shoulders to ease cramp. I see how they hold a quill in one hand, in the other a tool to remove any letter that goes awry, letters which are neater than my rows of seedlings growing out of doors, straighter than the stitches I make on hassocks. There is writing, scraping and sighing. There is no blood.

'I would like to try.'

I practise on wax and on fragments of parchment, the J of Jeanne and the U of Ursula and all the letters before and after and in between. Maude gives me a nod of encouragement.

When I tell Margaret, she smiles to herself over her embroidery, '*In the beginning was the Word.*'

I learn to cut pages and rule lines with an awl and am given a desk with the other scribes, showing my work every hour to a sister in the inner room who sniffs and tells me where I've gone wrong.

Before long my fingers are gnawed by the constant pressure, but my letters grow more obedient and I glimpse the perfection I could make. My heart begins to bend after all. When the flame of anger flickers, I quench it by night with prayer and by day with a new load of ink on the point of my quill. The idea of a beginning takes root in me, a new beginning in which I am unfettered from my past.

At Easter I am called before the Abbess who tells me I am to embark on a Gospel Book. My heart leaps at this affirmation of my skill but I lower my eyes. Our copying is an act of devotion and not for our own pleasure. I answer I will pray for the skill to bring this task to completion. I am taken to the library to look at other Gospel Books, comparing size and illumination, examining the pictures of the Saints.

I find Margaret in the narrow passage leading back to the cloister. When we are alone we talk in the English language. Although it's still awkward on my tongue it binds us closer, as if we were walking outside the gates, feeling the grass of the meadows under our feet.

When I try to explain this to her, she asks me if I still feel confined. 'Not so much, although I still wonder why I was brought here.' I tell her how I think the stranger may have fathered me.

'In that case,' she says, 'he only wants to keep you close. As God Our Father does.'

'But I will never know the truth.'

'Your lack of knowledge keeps you pure. All the same, you should confess your sin of curiosity.'

I don't resent her scolding me. It's what my mother would have said.

It is many weeks and the swallows are arriving under the eaves before I am close to completing the Gospel texts and a new temptation arrives; to put something in the Book, to make my mark in it. My quill strays to the last sheet, which will be fixed to the board, to its inner corner, where a tiny letter could go unnoticed by the head of the scriptorium. I am stopped only by indecision. Should I write a J or a U?

Then I am told I may attempt the gold letters, capitals in a different style, requiring more weeks of practice. After the familiar bite of black ink, the gold paint slides like a traitor and I struggle to master it. The striving for perfection renders me placid, my mind and body spent. By the end of the day there is no place left for hoping or wondering, for secrets or for pride. I'm grateful for the silence of the night and the solace of prayer.

Just when this great task has come to an end, Margaret finds me. 'I am leaving Wilton. Our brother will take me with him to the Northern Kingdoms.'

I sense the empty bleakness of these unknown places, a godless wilderness, they say, devoid of the colour of stained glass or finely woven wool, lacking even the warmth of friendship. How will she bear this new imprisonment?

She reads my anxiety. 'I shall find contentment where I can.' But her stillness, like a dark pool struck by a breeze, has been ruffled. She is relieved of her duties and spends extra hours in prayer.

I ask Maude for leave to pray beside her. She frowns but makes a concession of a few hours. 'You have your duties to attend to. Margaret will find her own way back to God.'

I am shocked into a reply. 'Margaret will never question His will.'

I wait to be scolded but Maude only raises an eyebrow. 'Your loyalty does you credit. Your kindness to her is a blessing.'

I turn to go but she places a hand on my shoulder. 'The Abbey will make a gift to Margaret. I hear you have made the finest Gospel book.'

There is talk among the sisters of The Pearl being thrown back into a world too dark and tawdry for her goodness. As the time draws near for her to leave, we pray for her salvation.

But watching from the high window, as her entourage rides out in a grey dawn, I treasure the knowledge that in the fold of her travelling cloak she carries my Gospel Book. I let it go freely and don't regret that it does not bear my name. It contains a splinter of my soul, my old soul, bruised by anger, scarred by impatience, waiting to be forged again in the labour of the scriptorium. Margaret will know only it came from Wilton.

From now on the work of Sister Ursula will go forth to many places, to be turned by many hands and read in joy, in hope and in despair. For this I am grateful, and for my obedience I am granted a letter to my old home.

I take my quill and write,

My Dearest Mother,

The life of a nun is to be envied and admired...

Aurora

Francesca Carra

I press the blade to the edge of her belly button. Skin opens like butter. Two small incisions, no bigger than the nail on my thumb. I push the ports inside.

Gas, please.

And her belly inflates beneath my hands.

It is sweaty beneath the surgical gown and mask and scrub cap, which covers almost all my hair, but not quite. A curl has come undone, I can see it dangle at the side of my face. From above, the yellow light casts its suffocating heat. When I was younger, during an operation, I once fainted. Now, I no longer mind.

I push the camera through the port, into the pelvis.

It is the body of a two year old that is asleep under general anaesthetic. Her name is Aurora, Latin for dawn. I met her a week ago, when my colleague, a paediatric oncologist, sent her over as an urgent cancer referral. Acute B cell leukaemia, he wrote in his email. Awaiting chemo. Could you consider ovarian cryopreservation?

I angle the camera. There it is, a tiny ovary on the screen. I push it to one side, then to the other. It is no more than a centimetre wide, the tissue pink and healthy and smooth against my instruments.

Both parents came to the clinic with her. Her hair in loose gold ringlets, she slept in her mother's arms. She's tired, they apologised. Limp hands peered from the sleeves of a puffed coat on her mother's shoulder. Each finger well-formed, the creases deep at the knuckles.

This is their only child.

I explained the procedure and looked away when her father's lips began to shiver. The mother remained stoic.

You take the ovary, she repeated after me, leaning forward. You freeze it. And later you can implant it inside her, and she'll be able to have children?

Yes.

Before they left, she shook my hand fiercely. I was offering her a way to defy life, and she was desperate for it. Take care of our girl, the father murmured behind, tears dripping silently from his face.

I hear his voice as I pull out from the port.

Diathermy, I say. My own voice is firm. In the operating room, these details matter.

I slide the diathermy through the port into the pelvis, clamp it onto tissue. The familiar beeping of the machine, the smell of singed flesh. A few moments later, part of the ovary hangs loose.

People think surgery is difficult. It is not, and this feels almost therapeutic. I advance, clamp again, watch more tissue burn.

I think of my own ovaries, of the ultrasound scan last month. The cool probe, the gynaecologist shaking his head at me with the same non-committal attitude I used to deliver bad news to my own patients.

For decades, my periods had been a nuisance at work, the fear of bleeding through the tampon onto the celestial blue of my scrubs. The scarce hours of sleep, the meals of milky lattes, bags of crisps, biscuits stolen from the ward kitchen. I worked evenings, nights, weekends. I cancelled plans with friends, missed birthdays and funerals. And with the end of each relationship, I became more indifferent.

I can't do this anymore, the men would say, in these words exactly or a prolonged version. There had only been a few of them, but in my memory they became interchangeable pillars of flesh. Tall and thin or short and stocky, standing by the kitchen doorway or the foyer, my house or theirs. Sometimes it was more explicative. One told me he'd already fucked someone else. That was easier for us both.

Mark, whom I now scroll past photos of his wife and two children on Facebook, had been the most patient. Please, he'd said. I love you, and I want to see you. But I hadn't known what else to do. I remember that night, it was winter and the sky a single charcoal cloud that glowed onto the city as I made my way to the on-call. My feet dragging across street, up the stairs, to the changing rooms; the drawstring trousers pulled at my waist, the shuffling to clogs. My toes were cold, the plastic numb against them. In the white light of day that followed, at home, his side of the wardrobe was empty. The board games, paperbacks, paintings in the living room – gone.

The ovary is almost loose. I squeeze the diathermy for a final time.

The list began after Mark left. I was circling the edge of youth, but it was still possible to find them. Many whom I would only know by first names, colleagues or friends of colleagues, strangers who looked at me in bars, set-ups planned by my remaining acquaintances. They seemed glad that all I wanted was an easy fuck, although nothing scared them more, afterwards, than a woman in her thirties with no expectations. And as friends retreated to budding families I worked harder, covering for colleagues, answering bleeps in the middle of the night and coming into hospital for operations that could've waited until morning. I dreaded returning to my empty flat, the silence slippery as silk as I unlocked the front door. The dusty counters, and in the fridge, the single bowl of hummus thickening with mould.

The ovary falls against the flesh behind it. My scrub nurse has been watching the screen. She gives a little cheer and hands me the plastic bag. I push it in through the port, manoeuvre the ovary inside it. It is slippery, and it takes a few tries before it is in.

There were things that I always thought I would do. But tomorrow is already yesterday, and all that will survive me are the surgeons I trained, the lives I saved. I've learnt, in these years, that people forget. Gratitude, after all, is a short-lived emotion.

I tried to change my attitude. I flicked through dating apps. I asked a sperm bank for a quote on IVF. I attended my gynaecologist who took the blood tests, did the ultrasound. On the screen, my ovaries were smaller than they should be, homogeneous, with hypoechoic follicles. I knew what that meant before he told me.

Now, I pull the bag out from the pelvis. The nurse pushes over the trolley. I unclench the grasper, and the bag falls open onto the sterile field, the ovary looped inside it. I pick it up gently and deposit it into the cryo box. Someone labels the box with a sticker, puts it in its carrier, runs out to deliver it to the van downstairs.

I can finally unwind. I deflate the abdomen, remove the ports, suture the cuts that I made. I wipe crusts of blood off the child's soft skin. I rip my gown off and leave my operating room, it is already no longer mine as I tuck the disobedient curl back into its scrub cap.

Aurora has one ovary left inside her. It will be destroyed by the cycles of chemotherapy she's about to undergo. But she will survive. I didn't tell her parents, I didn't have to. I knew that the oncologist already had. Acute B cell leukaemia has good survival rates and hardly any risk of recurrence. She will live to become a woman, and one day, if and when she wants, this ovary will be placed back inside her. By then, I will likely be dead. Neither she nor her children will ever know my name.

Tides

Anita Goodfellow

I've always been good at reading the tides. My father taught me. From the moment I could walk he took me to the water and showed me how to fish. He was the best fisherman on the Trang Peninsula and, although I'm only a girl, I've inherited his gift. I've got his plain looks too.

After the big wave hit the shore nothing was the same. I had finished the long walk up the hill to meet Kai from school when the bird song stopped. The eerie silence was pierced by the scream of the siren. The wave didn't reach us on the hill. We arrived home, hours later, to hell. Nothing was the same. The houses had disappeared, reduced to piles of wood or gone completely. The palm trees had toppled over as if they were matchsticks. Only the mangrove swamp remained. I shielded Kai's eyes from the body parts which draped the battered branches of the remaining trees. It was as if the world had ended. Our world had. My parents were never found. We were on our own, my little sister Kai and me.

You have to watch the ebb and flow of the water to know the exact moment to wade out into its depths. Time it right and you get a net full of writhing fish. Sometimes the water reaches my neck and the huge net I'm dragging becomes heavy, but my arms are strong and I never lose my footing. When the tide goes out the sand flats are laid bare, displaying all kinds of marine life and rubbish – mostly plastic. I like to pick out anything useful. Once I found a cracked mirror glinting in the sun. I gazed at my reflection in the fractured light and saw the battle-scars of life with Taam. I slipped the mirror into my pocket. I've still got it, but I don't look in it; not any more.

With the water gone, the mangrove roots appeared in the muddy estuary, twisted and cavernous. It was a place I loved to play as a child. Now I sometimes think I hear the whispers of the dead, my father's voice among them.

Taam knew I was good at fishing. That's why he asked me to be his wife. So many of our people had been killed when the wave flattened our village. He needed me. He thought he was the perfect catch. There was no father to arrange my marriage. I had little choice – Taam knew that too. I thought I was strong enough to cope with him. I remember thinking that Kai and I would be safe with a man to protect us. At least I proved myself with my fishing skills and that seemed enough, at first. But, Taam wanted a son. And then the tide turned with the arrival of the tourists.

Now when Taam and I wade out into the sea, just before the sun sinks and bleeds orange into the water, we can see the big hotel. The faint clink of glasses is carried across the water as the rich European guests sip cocktails.

We watched the structure growing day by day, changing shape. Now, Taam watches the ladies as they stroll along the beach, their sun-kissed bodies in contrast to the bright colours of their tiny bikinis. I catch their scent on the wind and hear their laughter. I feel their eyes on my back. I know they take photos of me as I fish.

Kai works in the beauty parlour of the hotel. She's pretty and just looking at her long dark hair and almond shaped face reminds me of our mother. Sometimes Kai rubs oil into the bruises on my body. The liquid smells sweet and eases the pain, at least for a while.

Kai is clever too. She brings me half her tips when she knows Taam isn't around. I've seen the way he looks at her, like one of the village feral cats watching a mouse. Taam is still waiting for me to produce a child. He says I'm barren and he's married the wrong sister. Kai's all the family I have left. Taam doesn't know about the money. I hide it in my sewing box. It will come in handy one day.

There used to be more fish in the sea. Now we barely catch enough for dinner, let alone to sell. Our wooden house, which I helped build, sits on stilts overlooking the estuary on the opposite bank to the hotel. At night, when I mend the nets, I see the lights twinkling and hear the distant thud of music. As the nylon fibres bite into my calloused hands I wonder what life would be like without Taam. He never helps with the repairs of the nets; he calls it woman's work. Instead, each evening he disappears. He says he's working, but I know he goes drinking. And I know what will happen when he returns.

I followed him last night to the local bar. I stood outside in the shadows and watched as he chatted to a group of young girls from the hotel. Then one of them stepped forward and handed him a bottle. She wore a gold dress cut low at the back, revealing the sharp bones of her shoulders. It was so different to the long sleeved cotton tunic I wear and I imagined the soft smoothness of the fabric against my skin. As Taam and the girl walked away from the group his fingers crept across the delicate straps to the area of white skin, like a crab scuttling across the sand. She made no move to brush his hand away. I pulled back into the shadows, but not before I heard Taam tell her how well he knew the tides; how, if the moon was bright enough, you could dive and see pink corals clinging to the mangrove roots.

He came home long after midnight. As he crawled into bed I lay rigid, but he turned away and soon his drunken snores penetrated the darkness. He smelt of nicotine, but also of something else. I turned my head towards him and realised it was the scent of frangipani flowers, like the fancy soap the guests use at the hotel and Kai sometimes gives me. He complains I smell of fish. I've learnt to bite my tongue, hide my bruises and bide my time.

I wake with the sunlight. Taam is gone. I am late. Hurriedly I dress and gather up the nets. He's at the edge of the water and as I approach he flings a cigarette down and grinds it into the sand with the heel of his boot. I flinch as his hand comes towards me, but he merely adjusts my headscarf. We fish in silence for the rest of the day.

Later, when darkness has settled Taam whistles a tune as he moves around our hut. It's a full moon tonight, which means the tide will be high – a perfect night for fishing. The water rushing into the estuary will be teeming with fish. I turn back to our simple room. In the flickering candlelight Taam combs his hair with slow, measured movements. Our eyes meet. He smiles. He says nothing as he leaves the house and I watch from the door as he unties the canoe. Why hasn't he asked me to go fishing with him? I stand in the doorway as he disappears, whistling into the night. The reflection of the moon on the water makes it shimmer like fish scales. I go back indoors and there's my sewing box, broken, the contents spewed over the bed. On hands and knees I pick through the detritus of the broken mirror and plastic treasures. The money has gone. I grab the mirror, make to fling it at the wall, but my reflection stops me. I peer more closely and Father's eyes stare back. My father used to tell me stories, tales of sea princesses and monsters that came out of the mangrove forest on nights like these.

Slipping my bare feet into my rubber boots I gather up my nets, the coils still wet and heavy, and make my way to the water's edge. High tides can be dangerous, but I can feel my father's spirit as I follow a narrow path upriver and deeper into the mangrove forest. In the moonlight the trees look sinister, but I'm not frightened; this is my territory.

My feet sink into the mud and warm liquid fills my boots as I wade out into the inky depths. My clothes cling to my body and soon the water is lapping around my chest, but I know it won't get any deeper. The current tugs at my legs and something brushes against my thigh. The water is alive with tiny fish, but they are too small to eat. I usually set my nets in the same spot, but tonight I'm trying somewhere different. I make my way to the place where the mangrove roots form a deep cavernous pool and, if you're brave enough, you can hold your breath and dive down to see the luminous colourful coral that hides there.

The nets secure, I wade back towards the bank and wait in the shadows, my heart thumping in my chest. I hear their laughter before I see them. The moon spills light over their naked bodies as they stand in the kayak clinging hold of each other for balance, laughing as they are rocked by the water. I watch transfixed. Taam struts to the end of the canoe. He raises his arms high above his head then dives, his body making a perfect arc. His dark head breaks the surface of the water. He calls out to her. Her name is Natalie. After a few seconds she leaps from the boat, her small white breasts barely move. She surfaces with a shriek, which he silences with a kiss. Eventually, they pull apart. They swim together deeper into the mangrove forest. Her hair, the colour of the sun, streams out behind her as they head towards the nets. One tug is all it takes. Their shrieks of pleasure turn to screams of terror. I wade out to the boat. Taam's clothes are in a pile at the bottom. My money is in his trouser pocket as I had known it would be. I free the vessel and watch as it is swept out to sea on the current. I turn away as the estuary continues to swell with water.

No one knows the tides like I do; not even Taam.

Blood and Bog

Jennifer Armstrong

There is no space to put you in the overhead bin, despite it being – in my opinion – the perfect place for you. I lay you instead down at my feet, so I am forced to sit with my legs gaping open, the Ryanair trolley bashing into my left knee. The woman beside me keeps glancing down. I lean over to her and whisper, *serves him right for doing the dirty*. She turns to the window and starts humming. When we take off you slide towards me. I can hardly bear the load of you. Finally we are flying and tilt forward again. Still you take your time, to mosey back where you belong.

All this hassle to indulge Mam's wishes, desperate to scatter you across the 14th tee, so you can smell the salty sea air and be carried by the wind to the Nordic fjords. But it was me that had to go retrieve you. Now here I am, trapped, with the man across the way from me coughing and spluttering. The woman at the funeral directors was the same, feigning compassion and sympathy through showers of spit. I could feel her judging eyes, acting as though I should be ashamed for choosing Ryanair for such an occasion. It's grand, I told her, not to worry – should I run into any hassle with the luggage allowance, it will be a relief to abandon the remains of my brother on the asphalt at Stansted. You wouldn't mind that, would you? Your soul trapped for the rest of forever, watching planes come and go, waving off travellers heading to exotic lands like 'Alicante' and 'Benidorm'. In the end they gave me no trouble. I told the man at the desk what I was doing, bringing you home. Told him I have all the paperwork and handed it over, not trying to hide anything, not trying to conceal the evidence. Told him I paid for priority specifically for the urn. The audacity of some people. The audacity of Ryanair. His name tag said Gavin and I thought that suited him alright, he looked like Gavin, looked like someone who doesn't care in the slightest about me or you or whether the plane is going to crash or land. He didn't look up once, not even to pity me. Didn't open a single envelope but only scanned my boarding card and told me we're delayed, so I should probably consider having some lunch. I told him we were newlyweds, off to Ireland for our honeymoon. No smile or nod or even a glance.

There is an infant behind me roaring, teasing out my temper so that it takes all I have not to turn and slap. Thank God mine are young women now, old enough to feed and comfort themselves. It was the girls who gave me the Ryanair vouchers that were about to expire. Killing two birds you might say, and in fact you would say, like when you were 8 and I was 6 and we broke into Mary McIntyre's garden to steal blackberries and set free the chickens she kept in the hatch. The desire to let them free, to live and die on their own accord, greater than the pull of roast chicken and gravy you had been promised for Sunday lunch. Finally, you managed to convince both Mam and Mary that it was all a great misunderstanding. The chickens had somehow done it themselves, *just wee jailbirds breaking free*, and they both bent over with laughter. You always did have a knack for spinning a yarn, Da said later that night, holding your arm against the steaming kettle. You are just too soft for this world, Barry, he said, so you

130

must grow some fat on the muscle and muscle on the bone.

I hope you know it's been a terrible inconvenience. The administration, the legalities, the back and forth, communicating in what feels like another language, the world of 'shall' and 'pardon', 'hereafter' and 'forthwith'. Death is such a terrible burden for the living, and Mam has been no help to me. Crying into the pillow. Standing at the kitchen sink rubbing her tummy, as though the pain in her heart has sunk to the abdomen. It did not help the way you left nothing in print, nothing written down. No will or wishes or goodbyes. I knew when the phone didn't ring at 3.45 that Sunday as usual. I had a feeling then in my gut that we had already shared our last words. I had a feeling the last time we spoke, that you knew something was afoot.

I hate this plane and everyone on it. Would have got the boat if my stomach could handle it, but it can't and it hasn't since 1995, when you came and brought me over, and fed me Guinness all the way, roaring with laughter when it came out staining black the Irish Sea. It's negligence really, because I could have anyone in this pot with me, and Gavin didn't even check the paperwork. I have the death certificate that ensures it was all above board, the repatriation papers that are signed and sealed. No third-party involvement or foul play. Foul certainly was Gavin's onion breath and bloated cheeks. Smelled like something I remember or tried to forget. Somewhere in summertime when we were only young. Days and nights spent away from our beds, at the beach or funfair or down the town, sleeping where we fell at mates' houses or out in the fields when it was hot enough, having bags of chips for dinner, when we were told more than once to just get out, *get out*, Da used say, with that look in his eyes. I remember walking in the house after being out gallivanting, when Da was standing over her, his foot dangling, and then you went and vomited up everything that was in you, the stolen beer and whiskey and the onions from the burger floating across the lino. Having too much fun so we were, he said. We were always having too much fun for Da. Clean up this mess Barry, Da said as he slammed the door. Mam's blood and the vomit already mixing. You laughing through your tears and whispering with your sinister cheek – I will Da, I will indeed.

I told Mam I want no more blessings once these ashes arrive. We had a funeral mass last month and I said one was plenty, but she craves the order and ritual and everything in its place. I told her I have no interest in having the cousins call up again for a whole afternoon of eating food that I would be forced to cook. The problem is that she seems to have forgotten whole swathes of time. Nostalgic for when we were only wee babes and life was full and joyous. She wants to sit and reminisce and tell tales, tall and long and winding.

'Tell us now Marie,' cousin Angela says, four sherries deep, 'a story from when ye were young ones...the shenanigans ye used get up to?'

Mam there laughing, smiling, egging them on, 'oh sure they were wee divils so they were'.

As if she doesn't remember, as if we don't share any history at all.

This child behind me I swear to God. I'd have him shut up and glued to his seat if he was mine. I want to catch his arm and show him your ashes, tell him that's what will happen to him if he continues kicking. I contain myself, but you know the way impulses overwhelm, to harm and hurt and tell lies. It's in our genes, I suppose. The number of times, walking with Mam when she is going on and on, I imagine swinging out my hips, just gently to the right, letting her fall just a fraction into the oncoming bus. The things we know we should not do or might regret terribly if we did, but still, take all our will to resist. Sometimes it's impossible to fight the urge, when it builds up, overpowers, consumes. Looking back I find it's hard to know for sure what really happened and what we tell ourselves, of our own misconduct. Sometimes we convince ourselves so well of things we forget there was ever a lie.

And I have to keep lying to Mam, because she keeps begging me to move back West from Dublin, now my girls are grown and their father is dead, and I'm practically an old woman myself, so she says. She wants me to be there for her when she is old and sick and can't look after herself. I tell her she is already old and sick and seems to be managing just fine. I tell her I have put down roots where I am now, and the grandkids are near me, and I don't tell her the real truth, that I would never move back while she is still alive. Only when she is dead might I manage to start fresh in that place. I might find I could enjoy the beach and the cliffs, the rock pools we used to climb searching for cockles and crabs. The charm of the coastal erosion, for what it offers me now, without being reminded constantly of the way things used to be. The way it all used to look so rugged and so handsome, when bare and untouched, before being shadowed with fencing all along the edge, with *Danger* signs saying *Do not pass*. Laden down with timber, haunting the lower dunes and crawling up to the spot where Da himself coughed and tumbled, his beer bloated body falling down the cliff edge and into the nighttime sea. Rocks invisible from up high, at that time of night, water so cold it doesn't bear considering.

My girls still talk about that day at the Blackrock amusements, when your pockets were replete with change. Decades gone now and they still remember it. We took the grandkids there the day after you died. I told them Uncle Barry went to heaven, and the wee one asked if that was far from London. I said probably not in fact, for you anyway, it was probably fairly close. I've decided I'll take out a wee spoon and scatter you there over the pier because really Mam need not know. Only so a part of you stays close to me, and so a part of you can sail yourself across the Irish Sea, back to London, if you wish.

Mam is driving to the airport to collect me. I pointed out last time I was home that the side mirror was broken. She said she hadn't noticed because she doesn't use them. If she took a driving test she would certainly fail, but it wouldn't be the worst way for her to go. We walked the beach last week and she started going on again about the night Da died, how the wind must have been exceptional, must have been some special sinister magic manoeuvring his mind, to carry him drunk and disorderly all the way to the bottom of golf course, to not fall and collapse any sooner, but manage to make his way so far until he was teetering on that lethal edge. Only one wrong step was needed and across all that land – 18 holes of manicured lawns and sandy ditches – he somehow managed to find it. She is obsessed with that spot. She says we must scatter you there because your soul will only rest if alongside Da, to be taken by the current wherever he was taken. She is sure you would want nothing more than to fall upon the rocks that broke his skull, ashes scattered like food for the fish that fed from his toes.

I tried to ask her soft and quiet, what are you really holding onto Mam, what about Da could you possibly miss? She goes quiet then, hums. Sings a hymn, *how great thou art*. Finally she says we must hurry back to the car, it's due to rain. I look up and breathe. Sky as blue as her cheeks used to be, after Da had had his fun. As blue as you might have felt, at the end, without me there to hold your hand.

It somehow feels now there is not long left of this. I always forget how short the flight is, how we take off and before I have even closed my eyes, we're touching down again. Nothing left of this last trip of only you and me. For so long it felt there was only you and me. Sometimes only just surviving, sometimes living so great it was hard to contain. They tumble in my mind, the years, fighting our way through endless dunes and rushes, me always chasing your tail, even when you got annoyed and shouted and told me *please stay home, please Marie, just leave me alone.* But I could never bear the thought of missing out, of you having fun without me. Even now I promise I won't delay, just keep an eye for me behind you.

The plane dives forward and there you go, this time sliding further away, pressing into the seat in front. I feel you slipping from me. I feel acutely the absence of you in this world, who was always there to mind me. I grab hold to keep you steady, to brace the fall. Keeping steady is essential in the face of these ferocious winds. Gales enough to lift you up and over, down into rocks sharpened by shale and shells and water. Breeze well able to knock you over, knock over even a full grown man, with belly and knuckles bloated and blue, water crashing down below, but, easier still, with a gentle push. Always easier with a gentle nudge, a gentle hand is all, to unclasp the lock of the hatch to let the birds run free.

Mam is so fixated on scattering you there, the cliff where he died, and it's not worth the argument or the back and forth. I'll stand there while she prays and sing a song for you in my mind, and for the two wee faces hiding in the dunes, smiling, scared, waving hello.

Through the window I see the land come into view, green

135

dulled by fog and mist. I feel my eyes itch and tire, a burden bearing down on my chest, a cold I am surely catching.

Vibrations rattle through the seat and into my fingers as I think to myself, who will mind me now? Who will help bear the load of these skeleton fragments caught between my toes?

The wheels touch down and I sense below the tarmac, centuries of blood and bog and stone.

Davy Jones and the SS Utopia

Based on the true story of the wreck of SS Utopia, 1891

Heather Child

I am a fisherman. Fisherwoman, I suppose. But instead of folding nets into my skiff and casting off onto the straits, I sit on our front step and mend clothes, working every day with needle and thread. When there are no more clothes, I go door to door, asking if there is anything else I can mend. There is always something that needs fixing in Gibraltar.

As I deliver ill-patched blankets and darned socks to my neighbours, I see Esteban and two of his cronies coming up Governor's Street. I know they will have dropped in to give my father his charity payment and to spread gossip. Sure enough, when I get home there is mud on the floor. He calls me to the side of his cot, which is made up halfway between the hearth and the privy.

'Pepa,' he says to me, 'They brought a catch to the market and sold every fish. Luis and the twins are going out tomorrow. You must go too.'

As he speaks, his hand emerges like a pale crab and takes the few pennies I have wrapped in my handkerchief, tucking them under his mattress. He has told me nothing I do not already know. Soon there will be no more charity, now people are starting to buy fish again. I remove my shawl, already sweltering, afraid that my father has made up his mind. Hesitantly, I ask if he remembers Tarifa, when the winds would not let us cross the waters and he told ghost tales to pass the time.

His face crinkles, not liking the tangent. 'What of it? Do you have the skiff ready?'

'It is ready, father,' I say respectfully. 'But I keep thinking about those stories, I keep dreaming of a metal box beneath the sea.'

'Are you still a child?'

He has forgotten how our eyes locked together that windy night, our beach-fire reaching from its pit in yellow ribbons. I listened hungrily, snapping up the scent of hell, as children do. He spoke of a mythical, bearded figure called Jones, who would tempt an innocent girl with promises of wealth and freedom, whisper into her ear and coax her into danger. Jones was in the glitter of coins, the dazzling waves. He was drawn to the wrong sort of thought – a selfish whim was a summons. Bad fishwives would find themselves tossed to the depths, as would girls who did not obey their schoolmistress.

I took the morality tale with a pinch of salt, not really seeing that I would have any need of education, nor knowledge of wifely duties. In my mind I was gleefully following the devil over bright puddles, along those tunnels I had explored so often, hoping to stumble on some long-forgotten pirates' hoard. When I stayed out too long, and my father found no dinner on the table, he would invoke Jones as he boxed me, asking if I wanted to end my days with cold salt water filling my lungs, the walls shrinking to a coffin. His words meant nothing back then, though the slaps turned my ears into seashells, roaring.

As my hand glides up protectively, I realise my father

has begun a rasping cough that pains us both. When he finishes, I say:

'I don't think I can take the boat. I've been having nightmares.'

'You need not go out at night.'

'It's just…'

'We cannot live on fresh air, Pepa.' He turns under the blanket, releasing smells of sweat and lanolin.

'I know, but…'

'Have you checked the nets?'

I nod. These last few weeks there has been little to do except repair our nets and do all those jobs we would normally neglect. We sit along the sea wall and weave twine, or oil our tools. Some fishermen have crossed the causeway in search of other work.

'You will go tomorrow.' The sound drains from his voice. I know better than to say more.

Though my hands tremble with exhaustion, I find myself leaving the cottage and heading up the slopes, higher and higher until I see monkeys foraging silently on the rockface. I used to spend time here as a child, when we played in the caves and raced to hide inside low-flying clouds. Since my father's illness I have always been down below, in the harbour or hauling crates to market. Casting off is the only thing I enjoy, especially if the straits are calm and glassy. I can imagine sliding straight across the sea until I smell the scorched chillies of Algiers, or the sweet Marsala wine of Sicily.

I remember my first time, that terrifying day I decided to take the skiff out on my own, telling no one. I kept the white wedge of the Rock in sight, fearing the currents. The nets tangled, and I could barely turn the winch. Yet later that day a whole school of herring fell on the deck, clattering and flapping. It was as good a catch as my father would have made, and I'd do it again and again. The fish don't know who is on deck. I took my herring to the market and begged Esteban to sell them, telling him how hungry we were. He looked at me for a long while, pulling at his black sideburns, and finally he marked the card *Jose Martín*, sold every fish, and delivered the takings to my father on his way home.

Although they are my livelihood, I have never much liked sea creatures. When I first went out in the boat, aged six, my father threw a lobster so its claws hit my bare feet and nearly broke them. Next there were two bass bloody from the hook, gills gaping, scales slashed. The creatures looked so confused at being unable to breathe. I wanted to toss them back, but my father would have whipped me.

His voice sounds in my ear. *You will go out tomorrow.* He is a hard man, always has been. My brothers were glad to escape his abrasive ways when they arranged their passage to Galicia. Now they both work in logging, sending home a small parcel of money from time to time. I envy them.

Imagine the whisper of an old voice, older than time. That is what comes to me tonight, dirtying my dreams as I slip inside a fissure and discover the haul of treasure: jewelled knives, Aztec spears and Chinese porcelain, all a little green with cave-drip but as valuable as the day they were looted. My ticket to a better life. I turn, hearing the door slam. *Let me out*, I cry. But Jones is the devil and never lets anyone go.

I awake sweating and exhausted, dragging the rag back from my window. I rake out the fire, put a kettle on the stove, unwrap a crust and cut it – no cheese today. I bring my father hot water, empty his chamber pot, change his candle and wrestle a soiled cloth from his fingertips. This wakes him and he gives a smile that sparks my heart. I turn away so he can't see my eyes filling with tears.

The sea is beautifully calm, and somewhere under the water the SS Utopia rocks with the currents. It must be nearly three months since this colossal steamship sank to the bottom of the harbour. I was out that night, and through the wind I heard gunfire, sirens and the cries of the passengers. Searchlights from our resident battleships picked out people clinging to the masts and floating in the sea, amid the debris of what we later heard were lifeboats crushed by a sudden list.

The next day, thirty-one drowned people were buried, along with two gallant sailors who had fallen in the rescue effort. But the ship was almost all steerage, and five hundred and three-score passengers were still unaccounted for.

Where were they? An uneasiness settled over the Rock. Business slowed at the fish market, imperceptibly at first, then falling off sharply. Not all the catch was sold, even at bargain prices. Why was this happening? I tried to find out from Esteban, grabbing his arm when I saw him in the street, trying to turn his hairy face towards me. He was sucking on a pipe as though he needed it to live. It turned out to be more horrific than I could have imagined. Someone had split open a fat red sea bream – the like of which I'd hauled in often enough – and in its belly had found a child's hand.

After that fish's stomach, no one had any more stomach for fish. We kept going out with the tide – a habit hard to break – but soon found ourselves throwing back any imperfect or cheap catches, knowing they would rot. We thought it would go on for a week or so, but two months later charitable contributions were collected to feed the fishermen.

The waves suck at the keel of my skiff, slurping and slapping as I make her ready. Dawn is breaking on the other side of the rock. Towards Ragged Staff I can see the steamship's masts poking up, a grim reminder of what lies beneath. I try not to look in that direction. They haunt me, those Italians who boarded a ship called Utopia, trusting the transatlantic steamer to bring them safely to their new life. Like most Gibraltar children, I had slipped aboard many steamships, expert at getting past the guards. The sailors were usually kind, lending us caps and telescopes for our games. I went down endless metal stairways to explore the steerage quarters, such tiny cabins, pressing my ear against the iron to see if I could hear the fish outside, wishing I could see through metal to the seahorses beyond.

My skiff is a cormorant on the waves. I feel the tug. A haul already – the fish have become complacent. Yet the winch is light and easy, rotating on its well-oiled gears, so perhaps not so many after all. When it rises from the water, I see a gelatinous mass. Jellyfish. Never before have I caught so many of these vile creatures, pulsing together, their bodies wanting to ooze through the gaps in my net. I lower them back towards the ocean.

Gibraltar is a grey peak in the distance. On the night of the wreck I was already at the sea wall, even before the crowds gathered. I knew the Utopia was coming and I wanted to be the first to catch sight of her. I had listened to that slippery, selfish voice and a plan had formed in my mind.

They say there were three stowaways on board. I would have been the fourth. *The wrong kind of thought.* Remembering my father's intonation makes me shiver. Was it me who brought this disaster upon them? Those Italians, hundreds of them crammed into steerage. It was the passage of the poor. They had no say in what direction the boat took them, no power to stop their foolish captain. They must have known they were approaching Gibraltar, steaming over that lip, that ancient waterfall where the Atlantic pours into the Mediterranean. When did they realise they were not going to make it? The metal would have screamed as the captain scraped past the HMS Ancon, opening his hull with its battering ram. Did it sound like the devil's horn to those inside, telling them that their time had come?

I can almost feel the water pouring into those small cabins, making people gasp and splutter like fish. Divers have been down, sure enough. They returned saying the bodies were packed too closely to separate. Men, women and children who boarded the SS Utopia hoping for a better life, but Jones took them all.

I have never been seasick before, but now I find myself leaning over the bow, head spinning. Eventually the feeling passes. I look past the reflections into the clear water.

Just below the surface, hundreds of ghosts are escaping the net.

Siren

Alison Jean Lester

It was a day like any other, Alana recited to herself on her daily walk from the subway to the ridiculous Frank Gehry designed building she was temping in. On some days it appeared to crawl toward her. On some days it recoiled. The rest of the time it looked as if it had been trampled by a giant toddler and forgotten. She'd said as much to her new supervisor, Marcus, when he'd asked what she thought of the place on her first morning there.

'It's an enormous, neglected toy,' she told him.

His eyes popped.

'And it's not as good as the Dancing Building in Prague,' she continued, 'and I don't like that one either.'

'Oh? What were you doing in Prague?'

'Dancing.'

'What, like – '

'Contemporary dance.'

'Oh! Do you still do it?'

Alana shook her head and looked out of the ridiculous recessed window, letting him imagine she had had to retire due to age – she was 29 – or injury. The window reminded her of the ones in her childhood copy of *Goldilocks and the Three Bears*. The chairs in Marcus's office were low, and now she was Goldilocks trying out Baby Bear's chair, folded down into it, worried she'd break it when she got up. That was temping in a nutshell: trying to find the right chair. When she looked back at Marcus, his eyes flickered away then back. He'd been appraising her body.

Now she strode daily past the guy she thought of as The Jiggler, a middle-aged man in a baseball cap who stood outside the building in the morning, jiggling his right leg, with a cigarette in his right hand and a huge mug decorated in pastel hearts in his left. *It was a day like any other*, she repeated in her head. The line was a sort of mantra, a reset button, the only useful piece of advice she'd taken from the therapist she'd seen after her breakdown in Prague. She opened the heavy door and entered the lobby with its walls coloured raw egg yolk, peacock and blood.

Although exceptionally talented, Alana had grown too tall for ballet by 16, too ungainly to lift, too much of a nail sticking up in any formation. Jazz dance also required physical parity, but contemporary dance didn't mind her height, and choreographers paired her with tiny dancers of both sexes, or men exactly her height, or had her serve as a structure to be danced with or even upon. She was happy to appear less than human in service to an interesting production, but it had meant being touched by all sorts of hands in all sorts of places. When a ballet partner's hand had touched her breast, it had usually been in order to help her down from a lift. It wasn't elemental, just practical. In contemporary dance, however, breast-touching was written in, part of being modern. It went with the semi-nakedness and the yards and yards of cloth, the pure white sets and the psychedelic sets, the water, the chalk dust, the shredded newspaper, the unidentifiable goo incorporated into the movement. It went with all the other discomforts, and Alana was intent on fitting in.

The dance they'd taken to the festival in Prague had been a nod to Balanchine's 'Prodigal Son', reinterpreted through the director's thorny mother issues. Petite adult dancers scaled Alana's body, but were never cradled. Alana's hands were to remain clenched in fists by her thighs, and she had to be strong enough not to stagger as one after another they climbed up and were rejected, climbed up and were rejected. Feeling proud, Herculean, she numbed herself to the hands sliding up over her nipples to grasp her shoulders for two nights and nearly all of one matinée. It was something she'd learned to do early in life during her father's visits to her bedroom, when she left her cold little body in the bed and floated into the air, secure only once her head bumped against the ceiling's cluster of fluorescent stars.

It was a day like any other when Marcus came to speak to her at her desk and rested his hand between her shoulders, with the pad of his thumb against the skin under her ponytail. *It was a day like any other* when she arrived at work three days later to find a small box tied with ribbon on her keyboard. Inside it was a pendant on a chain – a small, iridescent butterfly pressed behind glass – and a note: 'This made me think of you – M.'

She tied the box back up and took it to Marcus's office.

'No, thank you,' she said, and put it on his desk.

'But – '

'No, thank you,' she repeated, head high, scary solo over, and exited into the wings.

Jiggler, egg yolk, peacock, blood. The day Marcus breathed on her neck was *a day like any other*. Alana sat down to proofread an article on parallel computing, and on his way to get coffee Marcus bent down to see what she was doing, saying, 'Better you than me,' making himself sound cute and jokey to cause her to question the intentionality of the warm air that licked her skin. Then it wasn't like any other. On her way out for lunch she saw her dead father in the crowded, mirrored elevator. He wasn't looking at her. He had his eyes closed. He'd always had his eyes closed.

Alana sat at a coffee shop with a sandwich she couldn't eat and looked out of the window at the office. The Dancing Building in Prague was much more coherent, but still deeply silly. Frank Gehry had thought of it as the Fred and Ginger building. Presumably Fred was the boxy upright part and Ginger was the fluid part with the waist nipped in by an Astaire arm as she leaned away, as in the final spinning moments of 'Waltz in Swing Time', the only part of that joyful dance when Ginger's breasts are pressed at length against Fred and the dancers keep tapping and turning without breaking apart, and Fred's got his chin tipped up, looking into the corners of the room, and Ginger looks at him adoringly, but neither of them is sexy, he's got an energetic grandpa body, and she's never allowed to blossom, and they spin, and smile, and then suddenly the waltz is wrapping itself up, and you can see Fred, suddenly steely and determined, mark his target behind the sheer, stage-left curtain, and the spin gets faster and he stops smiling and whisks Ginger away and you can't see her expression.

The next day, *like any other, like any other, like any other,* The Jiggler looked Alana in the eye over his mug. The building exhaled on her as she pushed through the door into egg yolk, peacock, blood. She took the stairs to avoid the elevator. Less than two weeks remained on her contract. She could numb herself. She could stand strong, fists clenched, see it out. She tidied the final paragraphs of the parallel computing article and moved on to the letter from Marcus to all students awarded summer internships. In the

148

toilet after lunch, she saw her father's face looking back at her from the shiny paper-towel dispenser. *It was a day like any other.*

She waited until the end of the day to email her work to Marcus, then slipped out of the building down the stairs.

The following morning, The Jiggler was holding a different mug. Instead of rows of hearts, it said WORLD'S BEST MOM. He didn't acknowledge Alana as she passed, but before she got to the door of the building, she turned and went back to stand in front of him. He was drinking deeply, the oversized mug covering his face. His right leg stopped moving while he drank, then picked up again when he lowered the mug. Alana towered over him, and he looked up only with his eyes, took a drag on his cigarette.

'What happens if you stop your leg?'

'Say what?'

'If you stop your leg moving and stand perfectly still, what happens?'

'Oh.' He shrugged. 'I don't know.'

Alana watched his leg again as he took another drag, then she lifted her left foot and extended it slowly toward his right knee, slowly enough for him to stop her if he wanted to. She pressed the toe of her ballet flat against his patella. Controlling his knee, keeping his leg calm, she looked at his face. His eyes stared off to his right, alert to his own internal workings, his body immobile for once, but thrumming. She removed her foot and returned it to the sidewalk. It took only a second for The Jiggler's leg to agitate the air again.

'How did that feel?'

The man slid his eyes to hers. 'Like I wanted to puke.'

Alana nodded, and he lifted his mug back to his face. She went inside the building.

Climbing the stairs, Alana considered what the world's

best mom might be like and decided she would be a protector. She'd have talons, and she'd have fangs, and she wouldn't give a shit how she looked.

Alana stopped before the door to her floor. *It was a day... It was a day...* It had been a night like any other in the decade of visits from her father, until he ejaculated on her for the first time, coming on her flannel nightie, on her butter-yellow sheets, moaning in a new way that finally released Alana's own voice. 'Ma?' she called through her open door, across the hallway, through her parents' open door. Open doors were the rule.

'What?'

'Can you get him out of here?'

The world's best mom would have got him all the way out of the house with strips torn out of his flesh, white bone visible. The world's best mom wouldn't have waited for him in their bed while he cleaned himself up.

Alana paced the landing by the door to the office as she had paced her bedroom before breakfast the next morning.

It was a day like any other.

She went through.

'Excellent work on that letter,' Marcus said in the middle of the morning, steaming mug of coffee in one hand, one buttock on her desk, thigh an inch from her arm. 'You totally saved me, moving those hyphens around. What are you working on now?'

'The algorithms syllabus.'

'And then mine, right?'

'Yes.'

'Awesome. Okay. Cool.' He stood up. 'Listen, there's something I'd love your advice on. Maybe at the end of the day?'

'What is it?'

150

'It's um, just an idea I have. Need a woman's thoughts.'

'Oh. Okay, I guess.'

'Awesome.'

At the end of the day, Alana waited until Marcus was hunching forward to read his screen and hurried down the stairs. She was turning between the first flight and the second, listening for the reassuring clunk-click of the closing door, when instead she heard Marcus call her name. He could see her. She tried to pretend she hadn't heard and took another flight, but he was in pursuit.

'Hey!' he said. 'I thought you were going to come talk to me.'

She stopped. The landing had a door, but she didn't have a pass to open it.

'I forgot,' she said as he made his way down. 'Sorry. Oh, well!' She grasped the handrail, making to leave.

'No! It's okay!' he said as he reached her. 'I brought the thing I wanted your advice on.'

Alana looked at what he was holding. 'Your idea is a shawl?'

'Yeah. For my girlfriend.'

'Oh!'

He blushed. 'Yeah.'

'You want my advice on it?'

'Yeah.'

'Okay. Well, it's very nice.' It was. Handwoven, obviously soft, sky blues and sea greens.

'Let me just see it on you.'

'Why?'

'I just, I'm not sure the colours will suit her, but if it looks good on you they will. She's sort of got your colouring.'

Alana stared at him. He looked sheepish.

'Please,' he whined. 'It was expensive. It could be an

expensive mistake. I want her to love it.'

Alana exhaled. 'Fine.' She reached for the shawl, but Marcus opened it out and moved around behind her before she could grasp it. He laid it on her shoulders, stepping closer to wrap it across her chest, then moaning softly with his lips against her shoulder, his hands sliding over her breasts. 'Doesn't it feel fantastic?'

'Get away from me,' she replied, fists clenched.

'But this is so nice,' he wheedled, snuggling to her like a six-foot baby.

Alana tried to shrug him off but he gripped her more tightly, holding his ground. Suddenly she was Balanchine's siren in 'The Prodigal Son', spreading her legs to drag her dried-blood cape through them like a river of rage. Alana bent forward, pressing her crack against Marcus's hard-on, giving him the wrong idea before grabbing his ankles and wrenching his legs out from under him. He let go of her and flailed behind him, reaching for the ground to break his fall but the ground wasn't there and his head went crack on the third stair down.

Alana dropped Marcus's ankles, watching the heels of his shoes clatter on the landing and then slide away as his weight carried him further down the stairs. Making her own way down, even as she felt the stairs under her toe, ball, heel, toe, ball, heel, Alana felt her head grow light as a balloon and drift up, up, up, in search of the stars. She threw off the shawl. She was twenty, thirty, forty feet tall as she moved through the choreography in her head, reliving gestures and shapes she'd watched over and over and over – the siren's seduction, domination, and absolute possession of the prodigal son as she drew him to her, climbed on him, slid down him, sat on his head, spread her vulva under tights and leotard to press down on his hair, scalp, skull as if to subsume him, as if to reverse his birth. Alana looked down at the man, his head at an unnatural angle on the bottom step, his arms and legs askew and useless. She lowered herself onto his forehead, his eyes, his nose. He twitched under her, and moaned. Dancers shouldn't moan. She covered his mouth and nose, pressing down with her open hands.

Dock Leaf

Avril Joy

Sunday, a morning like milk. I'm standing in the kitchen, the door ajar, pale sunlight sliding across the floor when my mother, Alma, hands me an envelope and tells me I'm to take it to Michael Fitzpatrick's house. The envelope is sealed. His name is written on the front in her handwriting which always looks to me like she presses too hard on the paper.

'Won't they be at Mass?' I say.

'Not him,' she says. 'He doesn't go to Mass these days. Hurry now, Marianne, before the others get back.'

I put the envelope in the pocket of my shorts and set off, leaving the house by the dark shared alley out into the light. The sun is already high, burning off the mist, sucking up the dew from the meadows. Gulls circle overhead and the air has the salty lick of the tide making its way up estuary and creek to the timber yard where my father is at work. Half a shift on Sundays is double time. There's good money to be earned in the yard and in the factories round about, according to him. Though not for much longer.

'We're on the edge of recession,' he says, 'whatever that means.' I imagine a dry, mountainous place like the pictures in my old Heidi book, but not with green fields, or goats, or cows feeding on lush grass. I imagine a place different from here, a place of rocky edges and precipices where wild animals throw themselves off cliffs into the sea. Like I've seen in the nature programmes on TV.

I don't like to think about it, except for one thing, that Michael Fitzpatrick could be one of those animals, that he could be driven to throw himself off a cliff, land on the rocks below and be drowned by a giant wave.

If you didn't know our estate, you could easily get lost because all the doors are blue and the houses are identical, just the other way around. Like the Betts, who live next door to us. We share the same walls which means we can hear them and they can hear us. I worry about this at night when it's quiet on their side but loud on ours. When my mother tells my father to hush, you'll wake Marianne. When they fight about Michael Fitzpatrick, only my father doesn't know it's him they're fighting about.

Sometimes Michael Fitzpatrick calls for my father and they go off together to drink at the social club which is past the timber yard and down the cinder track. This is how I know my father doesn't suspect him. The track runs alongside the creek. I go there sometimes to wait for the sluice gates to open and watch the water racing through like a wild river, the kind people go rafting on, white water, they call it.

White is the colour of the mice the Betts keep in their shed. Alma says the Betts bought their new sofa and chairs on hire purchase. My father disapproves. Don't get what you can't pay for, he says. Alma nods in agreement, but I get the feeling she'd like some, or even a lot, of what she can't pay for.

What gives me this feeling is the red Post Office book she keeps under my mattress, for a rainy day. For a long time, I thought this meant for umbrellas and raincoats and all the extra things you might need to keep off the rain. I don't know how I came to realise what it really meant. It just crept up on me a couple of years ago. Just as the knowledge that Michael Fitzpatrick was my mother's lover crept up on me and that nobody was supposed to know, especially not my father, nor his daughter, my best friend Bernadette.

From time to time now, my mother hints about going it alone, as she calls it. Though I don't think she would be, alone that is. She says, 'You don't need me. You'll be fine with your father. You're like him, you're a pair.'

I make my way through the estate to the recreation ground, cross the old railway line into the fields and take the shortcut in the direction of the Fitzpatricks. The sun beats down on the back of my neck and my hair sticks to my head. The path is overgrown, burrs and seeds collect on the bottom of my shorts and in my socks. There are brambles hiding in the long grass and thorns that snag my clothes and scratch my legs. I take my time tiptoeing through, but my foot catches on a stone and before I know it I'm reaching out to steady myself and I've wrapped my hand round a nettle. The skin on my palm turns an angry red with small, white lumps that sting. I make a fist and try to squeeze the sting away. It doesn't work. My eyes smart. I open my hand and rub and lick my palm to take away the pain.

You can't miss the Fitzpatricks' house. It stands on its own, practically in the middle of a field. It doesn't have a garden at the front, just grass and a car with shattered windows, and bonfire-piles of twisted wood and metal that look like junk. My mother calls them sculptures. Artists don't care about appearances, she says.

I know where to find him. He's out the back, in his shed which Bernadette calls his studio. The door is open. Sun shines in through the large window. Michael Fitzpatrick's shed is nothing like my father's. It's not dark and oily or full of rags and tools too heavy to lift.

He's standing at a long bench with his back to me, but he turns as if he senses me there. 'Marianne,' he says, and he smiles. 'Are you here for Bernadette? She's at Mass with her mother.'

I shake my head. My eyes fix on the bench, on a tangled heap of old paint tubes, jam-jars full of brushes and a coffee mug with a heart on it. Propped on a small easel is a painting of two figures on a long sandy beach. On the shelf above the bench are his coleus plants which he's famous for, as well as his paintings.

'I was just going to put Leonardo out on the grass,' he says, taking a box from under the bench. He slides the lid off, and the polished shell of a tortoise appears. He lifts the creature out, one hand stretched wide across its back. Michael Fitzpatrick has the hands of a giant. The tortoise's head peeps out from under the shell. It stretches its scaly legs.

'Would you like to hold him?' He offers the tortoise to me, but I shake my head and step back. It's not that I don't like tortoises, though I don't really know much about them, but my hand still itches and stings, and besides, its neck is wrinkled and it looks ancient.

I come from a house where animals are not appreciated. Not even goldfish and especially not cats and dogs which Alma hates. I dream about cats and dogs invading the house. In my dream it's my job to shush them out but I can never be rid of them because just when I think they've gone, they creep back in and I have to start shushing all over again.

I follow Michael Fitzpatrick and Leonardo out onto the scrubby grass.

'There you go, Fella,' he says, and sets the tortoise down.

We stand together, side by side, Bernadette's father and me. We stand perfectly still and watch as the tortoise makes his lumbering way in the direction of a rhubarb patch.

'He likes a rhubarb leaf,' says Michael Fitzpatrick.

I remember the letter then. I fish it out from my pocket and offer it to him. 'It's from my mother,' I say.

'Oh,' he sighs. He takes it and lifts the letter from the envelope. 'Why don't you tear off a rhubarb leaf for Leonardo and feed it to him? I reckon he'd like that.'

I do as Michael says. I pull up a rhubarb leaf on a green, stringy stem, and hold it under the tortoise's nose. He begins to eat. I wonder if tortoises go back as far as dinosaurs. They look like they do, though being so small and so slow they would surely have been trodden on. Maybe that's why they have a shell, for protection.

Michael Fitzpatrick finishes reading. He shakes his head and sighs. He looks sad as he folds the letter back into the envelope and puts it in his trouser pocket. He leans down and helps me feed the tortoise. 'What's that on your hand?' he asks. 'It looks nasty.'

'Nettles,' I say, 'I did it on the way here.'

He walks off down the garden and picks at a clump of green. I think he must be after another snack for Leonardo but when he comes back he hands me a leaf. 'It's dock. Press it on your palm. It'll help take that sting away.'

I do as he says. I press hard. The milky sap from the leaf cools my hand.

He smiles.

Just then voices call behind us and Bernadette and John-Peter come through the back door of the house, sucking on ice pops, followed by Mrs Fitzpatrick.

'Hello, Marianne,' says Mrs Fitzpatrick, 'have you come for Bernadette?'

Before I can answer, she says, 'Would you like an ice pop? Bernadette fetch Marianne an ice pop, will you?'

I see her glance at Michael Fitzpatrick. A shadow crosses her face. He smiles, reaches out and puts a hand on her arm as if he's offering her a dock leaf. I wonder what Mrs Fitzpatrick would say if she knew my mother was writing to her husband. I think about the shadow and wonder if she already knows. I wonder what Mrs Fitzpatrick's writing is like. I think it would be different from Alma's.

She stands waiting at the shared entrance between our house and our neighbours on the other side, the Merchants, who don't keep mice or cats or dogs. They're more the bible, prayer book and rosary type.

'Well,' she says. 'You took your time. Well, have you got anything for me?'

'No,' I say.

'Well, did you see him? Did you give him the letter? Was he on his own? Did he read it?'

'Yes.'

'And he didn't say anything? He didn't give you a note for me?'

'No. Mrs Fitzpatrick came back with Bernadette and John-Peter, and we had ice pops and played with the tortoise on the grass. I got nettled on my way there,' I say, and I hold out my hand. My mother turns away.

By the time my father comes home from the timber yard, the kitchen smells of smoke and ash and Alma is upstairs in the bedroom. He goes up. I hold my breath and wait for the noise to fall through the floors, but it's quiet, quiet enough to hear the gulls out on the estuary.

When he comes back down, he takes the Sunday roast out of the oven. He cuts off and throws away the worst

160

of the blackened meat, cooks up some potatoes and peas and we eat dinner together. My hand stings from clutching my knife. I put my knife and fork down. I take the squashed dock leaf from my pocket and rub it on my palm. My father watches in silence.

When we've finished eating he says, 'Best you go out and play now. Don't hurry back and don't bother your mother, she's not well. She's got a terrible headache.'

There are a few other kids on the recreation ground but none I really know. I sit on a swing, my bottom half-on and half-off. I push back-and-forth with my toes. I wonder what Bernadette and John-Peter had for their lunch and whether they'll be out later. When they don't come out and I grow bored of the swings, I wander off over the fields, killing time. I feel heavy and slow, like a tortoise but without a shell.

When I think I've been out long enough, that the worst will have blown over and everyone will be in a better mood, I make my way home. As I arrive at the back door, I hear voices. I push open the door and step into the kitchen. Mrs Fitzpatrick is standing by the table. She doesn't look like her usual self. The shadow is back and her eyes are red as if she's been crying. My father looks grey and his lips are pressed tight.

Mrs Fitzpatrick, turns to me. 'Hello, Marianne,' she says, but her voice is cold and faraway. Turning back to my father, she says, 'Well, I'd better be going.'

My father nods. 'I'm sorry,' he says. And again, 'I'm sorry,' though barely loud enough to be heard.

We stand in the kitchen and watch her leave. I wait for him to tell me why he's sorry. I wait for him to tell me what's happened but he only shakes his head. He keeps shaking his head and then goes off into the back room where he sits down in the chair by the window and disappears into The News of the World.

Minutes later, he scrunches the paper up, throws it to the floor, and makes his way into the hall and up the stairs.

Who knows what the Betts heard? It was loud enough, that's for sure. But the house is quiet now, apart from Alma's occasional, muffled sobs. My father is off out. He's gone to the social club for a drink. He's gone alone. Michael Fitzpatrick did not call. Alma has locked the bedroom door. I'm on my own in the front room, watching Sunday night TV. I have until nine o'clock, my father says, then I'm to take myself upstairs to bed. The adverts come on for Coca-Cola, for Branston pickle, and for milk, though what a man high-diving into the sea has to do with milk I don't know. I feel thirsty and my hand starts to itch. I take the remains of the dock leaf from my pocket. It's shredded now, full of holes and past saving, even so, I rub it on my hand. I think about my mother's pen gouging holes in paper. I think about unanswered letters, about dock leaves and nettles. I think, nobody should have to throw themselves off a cliff into the sea.

Joy

By Abi Millner

She probably looked different now. She must do. Maybe she was glowing. She'd heard people say that. She'd aged, the creases at the corners of her eyes deepening. Or it was stamped on her, emblazoned on her jumper just above the school logo. Woman.

So, she stayed, still leaning against the tree.

He went, and she stayed. Still leaning, looking up at the shedding limbs reaching into the dirty white sky. Like arms held up. Like fingers grasping. She'd not noticed the shoes tied in pairs in the branches before, hanging limp and weathered. Like someone had climbed up, left their shoes snagged in the tree, and kept climbing. Climbed into the sky, dove into the sky.

So, she stayed. Mum would notice she looked different if she went home. Mum would see it, stitched into her skin. She wouldn't like it. She wouldn't allow it.

That's why he'd said they should go to the top park. They should do it there, against the tree. It was well hidden. Concealed by a thicket of brambles that would bite at exposed flesh. Claw at bare skin. And no one really came that way after school now that it was getting darker earlier. The afternoon shadows lengthening, swallowing.

He'd said they should because that's what couples do. Real couples. How could they be a real couple if they didn't? If she didn't?

He had been her boyfriend now for 3 months, nearly. Her first boyfriend. He was only a bit older, only a couple of years. That was nothing really. Mum wouldn't like it. Wouldn't allow it.

Fourteen is no age, Joy.
You're just a child, Joy.
Grow up.

It was serious, and they were in love but the hand holding, the snatched kisses behind the Londis at the end of Park Road and the concealed texts she deleted before bed – before Mum checked her phone – none of that was real enough anymore, he said.

She noticed in the time she had been standing there, leaning there, the dirty white sky had deepened to a ragged grey. Heavy. Pressing.

She drew it in with every breath, face turned upwards, until her chest was tight with the weight of it. Her lungs filled with sky. Two magpies landed in the branches of the tree, caught in its fingers. Held. They spoke with one another in an urgent, raspy chatter. She couldn't quite make out what they were saying.

She used to climb these trees in the top park as a child. Used to race up into them. Who could reach the top first? Who could reach up into the sky first? Breathe in the sky? Breathe in the blue?

She probably wouldn't climb anymore. Wouldn't reach for the sky. Now she would stay on the ground. Lean against trees. Pressed to the roughness.

He'd held her there, hands soft as he moved over her skin. He'd kissed her there, breathed heavy in her ear. Told her to relax. Why was she so tense?

Chill out Joy.

There'd been a pain she wasn't expecting. A tightness. A sharp aching somewhere deep in the hollow of her. Maybe that was normal. Maybe that's just how it was.

It had overwhelmed her. Coursed through her body. She'd tried to hold it. Keep it behind her teeth, bitter on her tongue. But it had leaked out. Spilt out of her.

The tears were off-putting, he said.

Turn your head away, he said.

She did. She wasn't a child anymore. She was a woman. So, she'd swallowed the tears down. Swallowed the bitterness. And looked away.

Turned her face to the tree. To the earthy moss and the scent of the bark.

They were a real couple now. They were in love.

He went home and she stayed, still leaning against the tree.

Salt for Longing

Sally J Morgan

Lightning spikes through mountain ranges into forests and long flat deserts. The sky is beer-bottle-brown, and anvil-shaped clouds the size of cities fizz with internal flashes as our plane manoeuvres around them. Across the whole of America, as far as the eye can see, there are electric storms. We are too close to a seething mass of black cloud, spinning like a gigantic science-fiction planet. It pops with flashes of apocalyptic light. I imagine dragons and monstrous glow worms escaping from another dimension to put an end to ours. I grip Bird's hand and we both force smiles as a lightning flash illuminates her face.

'Hold on, Mouse,' she says.

We're on the third leg of a six-flight journey. Bird hasn't had nicotine since we left Miami; the place where my sandal broke and a woman with the biggest thighs and the smallest skirt I'd ever seen stood screeching on a chair, as an opossum tried to hide behind the inadequate trunk of a potted, plastic palm tree.

'What the fuck is that? WHAT THE FUCK IS THAT?'

How did an opossum get marooned in a black marble hotel in Miami Beach? Its pointy white head, its ferrety teeth, and its scared little eyes peeked around the pot plant. The lady with the massive thighs was juddering like she'd never stop screaming and blue and pink neon buzzed nauseously around the rim of the reception desk, sending strange illuminations over the face of the concierge.

He saw me staring and shrugged. 'There's a storm coming, Ma'am,' he said. 'Them critters come inside when there's a storm coming. Don't worry none, he ain't staying.'

I had never heard anyone say 'critter' outside a cowboy movie before.

Bird and I are trying to return to New Zealand after taking part in an arts festival in the Bahamas. As soon as we get back to Wellington, which has been my residence for twenty years, Bird will have to leave me to fly home to Glasgow. Her visa has run out. After months of living together in the shabby rented flat where my ex had dumped me and my things without warning, Bird has to go back to Scotland to apply for a New Zealand work permit.

We don't know what's ahead.
We don't know if they'll let us be together.
We don't know if this will happen.
But I think it will.
I think it will.

Two days ago, from the veranda of where we were staying, we first saw these storms which are now filling the sky. We were in a dilapidated fishing lodge on the shore of an unfashionable island whose industry was the gathering of salt. The storms were like fireworks in the distance, faraway glimmers off the Atlantic horizon. We were the only guests apart from two American fishermen who had come to angle for bonefish. They took their hired boat out before dawn each morning and headed across the pale turquoise waters to cast flies for the bony moon-coloured fish that we saw swarming around the hotel's little dock under torchlight one evening. Little schools of ghostly darting carnivores.

The winds grew a bit stronger every day, and the place we inhabited on this island was in-between and nowhere as the time drew closer for us to part. We shared our hotel room with a gecko and a cockroach. The cockroach was very big and the gecko very small and we wondered which might eat the other, or whether they might marry and have very strange children, like things from a Hieronymus Bosch painting.

At night we slept under a billowing mosquito net held aloft with parachute cord tied to the light fitting. Bird fitted to my back like a parachute pack for half the night, for the other half I did the same for her.

I dream of falling, and drowning, and the red cords of parachutes tangling us as we fall through electric air with our fingertips touching.

When we land in Houston the storms are still raging. They're so widespread and spectacular they headline the news. In the airport, people who seem to be eating as a recreational activity rather than because of hunger, are wedged into rows of metal and plastic chairs watching giant screens full of ripped up trees and broken buildings.

Bird is going crazy because she needs a cigarette so badly. She walks too fast for me to keep up, and I lose her for a while. I discover her covered in nicotine patches and manically chewing Nicorette gum outside a store teeming with grey faced travellers. She's on the point of tears. 'I fucking hate this place, Mouse. It's choking me.'

I hate it too.

Houston is a desert town but the airport has become cold. They are cancelling planes. They cancel ours. We're going to miss our midnight flight to New Zealand.

The desk clerk is short and confident. She says, 'Good

news ladies, I've got you on a flight to Sydney, then on to Auckland and Wellington.'

I pore over the tickets. They don't seem right.

The connecting flight from Sydney to Wellington leaves a day *before* we arrive. I explain that this can't work but she insists that I don't know how time works in the Southern Hemisphere.

'It's different down there, Ma'am. Their days are in a different order.'

Bird puts another nicotine patch on her arm and stuffs another Nicorette in her mouth, turning away as I explain that I *live* in the Southern Hemisphere, and know exactly what order the days are in. I assure the desk clerk that, although water might swirl down the plug hole the opposite way in Australia, time tends to move continuously in a forward direction there, and the ability to travel backwards through time is no more common in the Antipodes than it is in the U.S. of A.

The clerk bristles and adjusts her brightly coloured uniform jacket before putting us on the next flight to Los Angeles.

My face is burning red.

Everybody is very fucked off with everyone. Lightning flashes off the runways. Thunder rumbles like an earthquake that comes from above.

The LAX terminal is resonatingly empty. Our plane to New Zealand is long gone and the airline is required to find us a bed for the night. The staff are tired and grumpy and their shifts are coming to an end. They want to go home. They don't want this shit. Shutters are half down, uniform jackets half off. Smart shoes are being changed for comfortable trainers.

At the desk a skinny young man, still fully uniformed,

is being shouted at by a taller one while he makes rapid phone calls. We're given vouchers for pizza and cola that aren't redeemable because nowhere is open, and put on a coach that's driven through the rain to somewhere that might be anywhere.

'Sorry lady, your airline didn't confirm, so we gave the rooms to Delta.' The hotel receptionist smells of citrus aftershave and doesn't lift his head, 'Next please. Delta Airline customers only.'

'How do we get back to the airport?'

'Not my problem lady.'

My face begins to burn again. I inhale deeply. I haven't shouted yet, but I really think I'm going to.

As I ready myself, I feel Bird's hand move gently across my shoulder.

'It's ok baby, come on.'

We are abandoned on their concourse with a handful of others. No fucking idea where we are but at least Bird can have a cigarette now. She smokes three in quick succession. Her shoulders relax and her eyes brighten. All of me does the opposite.

An Australian alpha male takes charge and we hear him raging on his cell-phone as he paces up and down and flings his hands wide in bellowing indignation. Despite myself, I'm glad of his testosterone-stoked energy. I'm worn so thin that there's less substance to me than tissue paper.

Another minibus full of Delta passengers arrives and I'm amazed at the power of bombast as the testosterone man coerces the driver into taking us back to the airport. He's going to sue somebody, he says. The driver looks fearful that it might be him and says that we might as well all get in, as he's going there anyway. Testosterone Man fumes into his top-of-the-range iPhone all the way back to LAX, and when we arrive he's met by an airline employee who whisks him into a taxi saying something about 'one of the last hotel rooms in LA'.

Abandoned again. There are five of us; Bird and I, two Kiwi women, and a distinctly omega male in his sixties who is flying to Australia to see his girlfriend. He is handsomely greying, with the air of a reformed hippy. His clothes are casual but expensive and his body language is loose and unthreatening – until he sees that the shutters on all the counters are completely down and no one is there to help us.

'Goddamn it.' He prowls around the corner to the offices where a light through the window in the top of a locked wooden door betrays human presence. 'They're all in there, goddamn hiding!'

A man's face appears briefly in the small window. They lock eyes, jut their jaws and scowl.

'Open up and sort this mess out!' Omega Man shouts.

The man behind the door shakes his head and we hear his muffled voice. 'I'm not on duty.'

'Then get me someone who is.'

'No one is. We're done for the night.'

Omega Man loses it.

He beats on the door with the flat of both hands. 'GET OUT HERE. GET OUT HERE NOW!'

The sound of his palms striking the door reverberates through the empty terminal as sudden violence.

A woman in magenta lipstick and wearing an outdoor coat over her airline uniform appears from behind the door beside the shuttered counter. 'Are you folks all okay now?'

Omega Man starts hammering on the office door around the corner again.

'Sir, please sir. Don't do that. You don't want them calling the police on you, sir.'

He stops, startled by that idea. 'Why would they do that?'

'You're acting violent sir. Calm down and come away from the door. We don't want anybody coming down here with their guns now, do we?'

He raises his hands in surrender and backs away. 'I'm not a terrorist. I'm a disgruntled customer.'

'I can see that sir, but best not to take any chances.' She sighs almost imperceptibly, unbuttons the coat that she had only just finished fastening, and reopens the door beside the counter to usher us in. 'Sit down folks. So many planes cancelled tonight – there's hardly a bed in the whole of LA, but there's this one place that no one uses much. I'll give them a call. You might be lucky.'

We listen in to one side of a conversation that seems to be going well. She puts her hand over the mouthpiece. 'They've got two doubles. Anyone okay with a smoking room?'

Bird and I look at each other before nodding vigorously. 'Yes, we'll take it, we'll be fine with that!'

Omega Man gallantly cedes the remaining room to the other two women. 'I'll sleep on a bench,' he says, and wanders off.

A taxi takes us to a small motel within sight and sound of the airport, each clutching vouchers for ten-dollar meals that will supposedly keep us going until we board our next plane at midnight.

We smell the room from the outside. Stale and metallic, like a pub ashtray from the 1980's.

'You're going to like it,' the bellhop says as he pushes the door open. 'It's got a jacuzzi.'

And it does.

A plastic tub stands right in the middle of a cramped room that at first appearance seems to be papered with brown wallpaper. But it's not. It's coated in liquid nicotine. Dark tar pools on the ceiling and thicker drips run down the walls like patterning. All the flat surfaces in this room seem to have a layer of cigarette ash over them, a fine dust that has settled over decades. It becomes very clear why this is the last available room in Los Angeles. We have literally been given an ashtray to sleep in.

The two single beds have a table between them and upon it lies a Gideon Bible. I pick it up. The grubby corners of its pages are turned down on the grimmest parts of the Old Testament; all the places where their god is the most irrationally vengeful. It falls open on the tale of Lot's wife who is turned to salt for longing for the home she's leaving. Tears are salt. Maybe she just cried herself into solid mineral. At least salt would be cleaner than this.

'Mouse, this is awful,' Bird whispers, and her arms fold into her chest as though protecting her lungs. 'No one has cleaned this room since 1948.' She inspects some stub ends in a saucer balanced on the side of the tub. 'No, I'm wrong. These have been here since the Depression. We can't sleep here. This is a weird kind of smoker's hell.'

'We're going to have to.'

It's four in the morning. Only twenty more hours living the American Dream.

What *is* the American Dream? I'm looking so hard, but I can't grasp it.

All I can see is a sky full of static.

A place where dreams are cremated in flashes of lightening.

A vast callous emptiness.

The jacuzzi seems cleaner than the beds. We climb in. Its water is just warmer than tepid and almost soothes. When we were at the arts festival we made a short video about drowning.

My fear of drowning and my fear of love.

We stood in the waters of a small inlet called Lover's Cove, each of our wrists tied to the other's with red parachute cords. The red cords snaked across the cerulean waters like the thinnest of brushstrokes. We struggled towards each other in the waist-deep seawater and when we came together, Bird plunged me under and held me down, as had been agreed.

Salt in my eyes and salt in my mouth. The sound of salt in my ears. The sting of salt in the little scratches the coral made on my feet. Salt of tears subsumed in the salt of the sea. When I emerge, panting and flailing, the salt stays on my skin but her mouth kisses it away.

I don't know how this will work.
But I think it will.
I think it will.

AUTHORS

Kathryn Aldridge-Morris is a writer living in Bristol, UK. Her short fiction has been published in over twenty anthologies and a wide variety of literary journals, including Pithead Chapel, Stanchion, Fictive Dream, Fractured Lit, and Splonk. She is the winner of The Forge Literary Magazine's prize for Flash Nonfiction, Lucent Dreaming's flash fiction award and Manchester Writing School's *QuietManDave* prize. She was recently awarded an Arts Council grant to write her novella-in-flash. You can read more of her work at: www.kamwords.com.

Jennifer Armstrong was born and raised in the West of Ireland. She has also lived in Patagonia, Bilbao, Edinburgh, London, and is currently based in Norwich. She is soon to complete the MA in Prose Fiction at the University of East Anglia. In 2022, she was shortlisted in the Bournemouth Short Story Prize and was recently selected for the Stinging Fly Summer School with Michael Magee. She is interested in character as form, brevity in prose and the rhythms of language.

Ali Bacon was born in Scotland then moved to the South West of England where her writing is still strongly influenced by her Scottish roots. Following a contemporary novel, *A Kettle of Fish,* (Thornberry, 2012) she wrote *In the Blink of an Eye* (Linen Press, 2018) which is set in nineteenth century Edinburgh and was listed in the ASLS best Scottish books of that year. She has also had a number of short story successes and acts as occasional co-judge for the acclaimed Stroud Short Stories event. Ali's second historical novel *The Absent Heart*, inspired by the letters of R. L. Stevenson to Frances Sitwell, will be published by Linen Press in 2025.

Cath Barton is an English writer of Scottish descent. She won the New Welsh Writing AmeriCymru Prize for the Novella 2017 for *The Plankton Collector*, which was first published in September 2018 by New Welsh Review and given a special mention in the Saboteur Awards Best Novella category 2019. Cath's further novellas are *In the Sweep of the Bay* (2020, Louise Walters Books), *Between the Virgin and the Sea* (2023, Novella Express, Leamington Books) and *The Geography of the Heart* (2023, Arroyo Seco Press). A pamphlet of her short stories, *Mr Bosch and His Owls,* was published in 2024 by Atomic Bohemian. Cath now lives in Abergavenny in South Wales with her husband and their black and white cat.

Lesley Bungay was born and grew up in the Northeast, a Geordie at heart. She now lives in Hampshire with her husband, a little further from the sea than she'd like. She writes novels, short stories, flash fiction, and the occasional Haiku. She has short stories and flash fiction published in the print anthologies: *Swan Song* (Retreat West), and *The Rabbit Hole Vol.V* (Writing Co-op Production), as well as online at Wensum Lit, NFFD Flash Flood 2023, Paragraph Planet, 101 Words and 50 Word Stories. She won Second Prize in the Yeovil Literary Prize 2020 and two Third Prizes in the Hampshire Writers Society monthly competition. She has been short/longlisted with The Fish Prize, Writing Magazine, Cranked Anvil, Retreat West and Flash 500. Lesley is represented by Intersaga Literary Agency Ltd and is currently on submission with her debut novel, *The Year Without a Summer,* which reached the Top 100 of the Cheshire Novel Prize 2023.

Rachel Burns lives in County Durham and is a poet, short story writer and playwright. Short stories published in Mslexia and Signs of Life anthology. Short plays performed at Live Theatre, Newcastle and The Gala Theatre, Durham. She has been placed in poetry competitions including The Julian Lennon Prize for Poetry and The Classical Association Poetry Competition. She has been published in various literary magazines including Mslexia, Magma, The Rialto, Butcher's Dog and Spelt Magazine. Anthologised in North Country, an anthology of landscape and nature, edited by Karen LLoyd, Saraband. Her poetry pamphlet, a *girl in a blue dress*, is published by Vane Women Press. She is an alumnus of the Arvon/Jerwood mentoring programme. She received an Arts Council grant in 2023 and is working towards her first poetry collection.

Francesca Carra was born in Italy. She lives in London, where she writes short fiction.

Heather Child is a Bristol-based author who grew up in the Midlands. Her two novels, *Everything About You* and *The Undoing of Arlo Knott,* are published by Orbit Books. Her award-winning short stories have appeared in various magazines and anthologies, and she is a member of Just Write Bristol. Follow Heather on X: @Heatherika1 or visit her website: www.heather-child.co.uk.

Susan Clegg's first novel, *The Dolphin*, was published by Linen Press in 2023. Her short stories have been published in Matter magazine and The Stinging Fly and the story,

Dogwood, was shortlisted for the Royal Society of Literature V. S. Pritchett Short Story Prize. She lives in Sheffield and is a graduate of the Hallam University MA Writing programme.

Mona Dash is an award-winning author based in London. Her work includes her memoir A *Roll of the Dice,* a short story collection *Let Us Look Elsewhere*, a novel *Untamed Heart* and two collections of poetry, *A Certain Way* and *Dawn Drops*. She has been published in various journals and more than thirty-five anthologies. Her short stories have been listed in leading competitions such as Asian Writer (winner), Bath, Bristol, Fish to name some. She has been shortlisted, and more than once, in various literary awards such as Eastern Eye ACTA, SI Leeds Literary award, Eyelands Literary Award (winner for *Roll of the Dice*) Tagore Literary Prize and Novel London. Her short story *Twenty-five years* was presented on BBC Radio 4 and the title story *Let Us Look Elsewhere* was included in Best British Short Stories '22. She also works as a business leader in AI for a global tech company. A brief appearance in the TV series *Silverpoint* (CBBC, BBC iPlayer) has her reminiscing about different careers! www.monadash.net, Instagram at @monadash_

Anita Goodfellow has an MA in creative writing from Bath Spa University. Her work has been placed and shortlisted in various competitions including Flash 500, Retreat West, Trip Fiction, Evesham Festival of Words, Cranked Anvil, Bath Flash Fiction Award and The Bedford Competition and published in numerous anthologies including The National Flash Fiction Day Anthology 2024, *Tiny Sparks Everywhere*. She is a reader for The Bedford Competition. She is currently finalising her debut novel, *So We Might As*

Well Dance and putting together a short story collection, *The Pigeon Wallah and Other Stories*. @nitagoodfellow

Avril Joy Before becoming a full-time writer, Avril Joy worked for twenty-five years in a women's prison in County Durham. Her short fiction has appeared in literary magazines and anthologies, including Victoria Hislop's *The Story: Love, Loss & the Lives of Women*. Her work has been shortlisted in competitions including the Bridport and the Manchester Prize for Fiction. In 2012 her short story, *Millie and Bird* won the inaugural Costa Short Story Award. Her novel, *Sometimes a River Song*, published by Linen Press, won the 2017 People's Book Prize. Her poem, *Skomm* won first prize in York Poetry Comp and appeared in *The Forward Book of Poetry 2019*. Her latest novel is *The Silent Women. Dock Leaf* is previously unpublished.

Alison Jean Lester is the author of one short-story collection, *Locked Out: Stories Far from Home,* and has also had stories published in *Good Housekeeping, Barrelhouse, Synaesthesia, On the Seawall,* and *Ecotone*. Her first novel, *Lillian on Life*, was published in 2015, followed by *Yuki Means Happiness, Glide,* and *The Sound of It*. She also writes non-fiction. Her memoir, *Absolutely Delicious: A Chronicle of Extraordinary Dying,* discusses three deaths in her family, and her essay collection, *Restroom Reflections: How Communication Changes Everything,* offers thoughts from her career as a corporate communication-skills coach. She is the product of a British mother and an American father, and has been living in Worcestershire since 2016, after 25 years in Asia.

Maria C. McCarthy was born in 1959 and raised in a community of Irish migrants in Epsom, Surrey. Her Irish heritage features strongly in her writing. She is the author of two poetry collections: *strange fruits* and *There are Boats on the Orchard*; a collection of linked short stories, *As Long as it Takes*; and is contributing editor of *Unexplored Territory*. All four books are published by Cultured Llama. She is also a contributing editor of *Inspired by Six Women Who Shook the World* (Medway Libraries). Maria was the winner of the Society of Authors' Tom-Gallon Trust Award 2015 for her short story *More Katharine than Audrey*. In 2011, she co-founded Cultured Llama Publishing with her husband, Bob Carling, and was poetry and fiction editor for the lifetime of the press. She has an MA with distinction in Creative Writing from the University of Kent. She lives in the Medway Towns. Her latest publication is Inspired by Six Women who Shook the World , edited by SM Jenkin and Maria C. McCarthy.

Margot McCuaig was born in Scotland but built a home on her father's farm in Rathlin Island, Ireland, where she finds constant inspiration. She writes literary fiction and her acclaimed debut novel, The Birds That Never Flew, was shortlisted for the Dundee International Book Prize and longlisted for the Polari Prize. Her second novel, Almost Then, 'skilful... tense and tender in equal measures' (Scotsman, Book of the Week), was published in 2021. She also writes fiction and creative non-fiction, short stories, and is published in the Federation of Writers (Scotland) 2024 anthology and by Luath Press. She is an award winning documentary filmmaker, and won Royal Television Society Scotland awards for her documentary films in 2015, 2016, 2019 and 2021. She is currently writing a PhD; an autoethnography – examining gender, class and emotion in her films.

Abi Millner was born and raised in Dorset. She has completed a BA Hons degree in Creative Writing, during which she discovered a love for short and flash fiction. Her short story *Joy* was part of her degree Major Project, a collection of literary, and experimental short stories titled *One for sorrow*. Featuring in the Linen Press anthology, *Joy* is Abi's first published work. She now lives in the Peak District with her husband and children, and will complete her master's degree in creative writing in 2025.

Sally J Morgan is a published author and an internationally exhibited artist. She was born in Wales and grew up in Yorkshire. Her novel, *Toto Among the Murderers* (John Murray) won the Portico Prize in 2022. Sally went to art school in Sheffield and Antwerp, achieved an MA in History from Ruskin College, and has a PhD in Creative Practice from Deakin University, Melbourne. She has had chapters, articles and creative writing in various publications including Landfall Literary Journal, the Guardian, and the Irish Times. After living for many years in New Zealand, she and her wife returned to the UK to settle in West Yorkshire in 2022.

Jess Richards was born in Wales and raised in Scotland. She is the author of three literary fiction novels: Costa shortlisted *Snake Ropes, Cooking with Bones* and *City of Circles* (Sceptre). She also writes creative nonfiction, vispo, short fiction and poetry which have been published in various anthologies. Her fine art / creative writing PhD project, *Illusions, Transformations, and Iterations; storytelling as fiction, image, and artefact*, earned her a place on the Dean's List at Massey University, Aotearoa New Zealand. *Birds and Ghosts* (Linen Press) is a book-length work of creative nonfiction written when New Zealand borders were closed due to Covid19. In October

2022 Jess, her wife, and two stripy cats returned to live in the UK. They now live in Yorkshire where Jess works at the University of Leeds.

Shelley Roche-Jacques' work has appeared in magazines and journals such as *The Boston Review, Litro, Flash: the International short-short story magazine, Magma* and *Brevity*. Her poetry pamphlet *Ripening Dark* was published in 2015, followed by a collection of dramatic monologues, *Risk the Pier*, in 2017. Her work has been highly commended for the Bridport Prize and shortlisted for the Bath Flash Fiction Award and the *Wigleaf Top 50*. As a researcher, she is interested in the idea of flash fiction as a distinct literary form. She teaches Creative Writing at Sheffield Hallam University, where she is Course Leader for the BA Creative Writing and MA Creative Writing programmes.

Reshma Ruia was born in India, raised in Italy and now lives in Manchester. Her first novel, *Something Black in the Lentil Soup*, was described in the Sunday Times as 'a gem of straight-faced comedy'. She has published a poetry collection, *A Dinner Party in the Home Counties*, winner of the 2019 Word Masala Award. Reshma's work has appeared in anthologies and journals, and has been commissioned by the BBC, University of Cumbria and Manchester Literature Festival. She is the co-founder of The Whole Kahani – a writers' collective of British South Asian writers. www.reshmaruia.com

Anna Sansom is a queer midlifer who writes fiction and creative non-fiction. Much of her work focuses on writing about 'imperfect intimacy' and creating 'expansive erotica'. She wrote the Sex/Life pages for DIVA Magazine (the leading magazine for LGBTQIA+ women and non-binary people) for two years. Her short stories have been published in several anthologies (including *Best Women's Erotica of the Year, Volume 10*, Cleis Press, *The Big Book of Quickies*, Cleis Press, and *I Write the Body*, Kith Books). Other publications include her more-than-a-memoir, *Desire Lines* (The Unbound Press), and her novel, *Coming Close* (Xcite Books). She has a Substack account where she shares her 'living experiment of desire in queer midlife' (annasansom. substack.com). She is the editor and curator of an anthology of personal essays and speculative fiction written by international authors (*Sex Meets Life*). Anna loves tea, swimming in the sea, and talking to her cats. Find her at annasansom.com

Catherine Smith was born and raised in Windsor, and educated at the Universities of Bradford and Sussex. She is the author of three full poetry collections – *The Butcher's Hands, Lip* and *Otherwhere* (Smith Doorstep); two pamphlets, *The New Bride* (Smith Doorstop) and *The New Cockaigne* (The Frogmore Press); and one collection of short stories, *The Biting Point* (Speechbubble Books). Two of her poetry publications have been short-listed for Forward Prizes, and in 2004 she was selected as a 'Next Generation' poet by the Arts Council/Poetry Book Society. Her poetry and short fiction have been broadcast on BBC Radio 4, included in anthologies and adapted for Live Literature performances. She tutors for The Poetry Society and The Arvon Foundation and is also a freelance mentor/ editor. She lives in Lewes, East Sussex, with her husband and cat, and is currently writing (and re-writing) short stories and a supernatural,'domestic noir' novella.

Emma Timpany was born and grew up in the far south of Aotearoa New Zealand. She is the author of the novella

Travelling in the Dark (Fairlight Books) and of short story collections including *Three Roads* (Red Squirrel Press). Emma edited and co-edited the anthologies *Botanical Short Stories* and *Cornish Short Stories* (The History Press). Her writing has won awards including the Hall and Woodhouse DLF Writing Prize and the Society of Authors' Tom-Gallon Trust Award. *Impressionism* was published previously in the literary journal *Meniscus* and in *Three Roads*. Emma lives with her family in Cornwall.

Kate Vine is an author and freelance writer living in York. She has an MA in Creative Writing from the University of East Anglia. Her short fiction has been published widely including *This content has been removed* published in *Lunate* Vol. 2 (2023), *The Colour of Sunflowers* published in *The Word for Freedom* (2018) and *Anatomy* published in *Permanent Emotion* (2024). Her fiction has also won the Lunate 500 competition and been shortlisted for the Bath Short Story Award 2019. She is represented by Charlotte Seymour at Johnson & Alcock for her debut novel.

ACKNOWLEDGEMENTS\

Ali Bacon. *Within These Walls* won the Bristol Short Story Competition Sansom (Local Writer) Prize in 2019.

Rachel Burns. Snowdrops was first published in Signs of Life – an anthology edited by Sarah Sasson, MoshPit Publishing.

Lesley Bungay. *The Last Walk* was first published in *Time, H.G. Wells Short Story Competition 2019* (St Ursin Press).

Heather Child. *Davy Jones and the SS Utopia* was originally published in Mslexia, the magazine for women who write, mslexia.co.uk.

Maria C. McCarthy. *Cold Salt Water* was winner of the Save As Prose Awards, 2009, and has previously been published in *The Frogmore Papers*, Issue 75, Spring 2010, in the anthology *Unexplored Territory* (Cultured Llama, 2012), on the website *East of the Web*, and in Maria's short story collection, *As Long as it Takes* (Cultured Llama, 2014).

Anita Goodfellow. *Tides* was awarded second place in the Flash 500 short story competition in January 2020 and is published on their website.

Reshma Ruia. *My Mother's Twelfth Suitor* first appeared in her short story collection, *Mrs Pinto Drives to Happiness,* shortlisted for the 2022 Eastern Eye ACTA Awards. Her new novel, *Still Lives* won the 2023 Diverse Book Readers' Choice Award.

Emma Timpany. *Impressionism* was published previously in the literary journal *Meniscus* and in *Three Roads*.